Also by Robert Statzer

Dark Harvest

Death is Not Enough

To Love A Vampire

Robert Statzer

For Ingrid Pitt
1937 – 2010

Contents

Introduction

Vampires. For generations these creatures from folklore have had a tremendous impact on pop culture, be it merchandise, the printed word or the silver screen. To this day Bram Stoker's classic novel *Dracula* (1897) remains one of the best-selling books of all time, while Sheridan Le Fanu's Victorian vampire tale "Carmilla" (1871) continues to be a staple of short story anthologies. And both have been the direct (or indirect) inspiration for countless film and television offerings. Why do they remain so popular? Perhaps it is because they are one of the few shared superstitions; even in ancient times, variations on the vampire legend could be found in nearly every culture around the world. And they come in all shapes and guises, be it predator, seducer or sympathetic victim of circumstance. Over the years, many readers have wondered why a scientist like Dr. Van Helsing was one of the first characters in *Dracula* to suspect that a supernatural creature stalked the streets of London. Let us look back at Van Helsing's initial encounter with the occult, during his years as a young medical student....

Robert Statzer
June 8, 2018

1. Hell's Belles.

A brisk breeze swept through the cemetery trees, scattering their remaining leaves and sending them whispering in the cool November night as they spiraled down to dance across the ground. Leaning back in his saddle, General Spielsdorf looked up at the dark clouds carried across the moon by the wind. A storm was moving in, he could both feel and smell it in the air. Even the elements had been allied against him and his men. The chill went deep into his bones, making him feel older than his 60 years, and the sharp sting of the air made his eyes water.

Swinging down from the saddle, Spielsdorf cocked his pistol crossbow and took a wooden bolt from the leather pouch he wore at his waist, inserting it into the weapon. While the wood alone should make it fatal enough for his prey, he had taken the precaution of dipping the tip of each projectile in holy water earlier that evening. After the attack on his family, he was leaving nothing to chance. His quarry had been clever, seeking refuge in the cemetery. There were hundreds of graves they could hide in, knowing it would be impossible for Spielsdorf's soldiers to search them all.

As Spielsdorf moved quietly along the crumbling wall of an ancient crypt, his eyes and ears strained for any sign of activity from his men or from the three women they had tracked to the forgotten graveyard. The stones were stained with age, and vein-like vines crept across their jagged surface. The crunch of footsteps on dried leaves came from behind and Spielsdorf turned to see a blur of fur hurtling toward him. The werewolf slammed into the general, knocking him to the ground.

Straddling the downed man, the beast reared back to howl in triumph. Its victory cry was cut short by two silvered blades flashing in the moonlight as they severed the creature's head from its neck. The dead beast's body slumped to one side as its head rolled away in the opposite direction, each returning to human form as life left them. Standing over Spielsdorf stood Lieutenant Markus, black blood dripping from the curved Kukri knives held in each hand. Tossing one blade to stick into the ground, he offered the general his newly freed hand and helped him to his feet.

"Thank you, lieutenant," Spielsdorf said. "I'm afraid I didn't count on Countess Bathory having a guard dog with her."

Markus held up the dead man's head. "I know this one," he said. "It's Albrecht…or, at least, was."

Spielsdorf grew grim. "One of our own men."

Tossing the head aside, Markus picked up the discarded Kukri knife. "What would cause a man to turn against his own kind?"

Faint laughter echoed in the night, soft and unsettling, followed by a female voice that answered his question with a question. "Perhaps the promise of eternal life…and eternal love?" Like a living mist the ghostly form of a young woman with long auburn hair appeared in the moonlight, her shape taking on substance to stand before them as flesh and blood.

"Carmilla," Spielsdorf said beneath his breath.

There was a look of contempt for Spielsdorf in the girl's eyes at the sound of her name on his lips. Her tone and expression softened as she returned her attention to Markus, slowly approaching him as she spoke. "And what about you, my handsome young lieutenant? Have you any ambitions beyond losing your life in some noble battle?"

Markus smiled. "My ambition is to win, not to lose."

Carmilla now stood directly before Markus, gently slipping her arms around him. "No matter whether you're in bed or on the battlefield, Death will one day come for you. I can prevent that. You'll never be touched by time or disease." She tilted her head back, offering her mouth to his and spoke softly. "Let me feel the heat of your body warm mine."

Markus was unable to look away from her gaze and felt drawn to her in spite of himself. As their lips brushed against each other, Spielsdorf cried out, "No, Markus; don't let her kiss you!" Making the sign of the cross, the older officer commanded "*Diabolus absum.*"

The supernatural reverie broken, Markus shoved her away. Carmilla's eyes blazed red as she whipped her head around to glare at Spielsdorf. Before she could lash out at the older man, Markus sprang forward with the Kukri knives. With catlike reflexes, Carmilla twisted away from the oncoming blades. Although neither knife made its way into her heart, one plunged deep into her shoulder as she tried to dart out of their path and her blood gushed across Markus' forearm.

"Bastard!" Carmilla spat the word at him as she clutched her wound. "I could have given you endless youth."

"As what?" Markus asked with a nod toward the lifeless body of the werewolf he had just slain. "One of your lap dogs?" With the loss of blood Carmilla began grow older; prompting the officer to observe, "I do believe you're starting to look a bit long in the tooth."

Spielsdorf's arm whipped up, the crossbow pistol ready to finish what Markus' knives had failed to do. As he squeezed the trigger Carmilla sprang into the air, her shroud sweeping out about her as her shape shifted, shrinking into that of an enormous bat with a wingspan as wide as a man's outstretched arms. The arrow whizzed past her, projectile and intended target both vanishing into the night. Markus started to move off in the direction the bat flew, but stopped at the sound of Spielsdorf's voice.

"Forget about her; she won this time."

"Do you think she might bleed to death?"

"No," Spielsdorf said, shaking his head. "By now the wound will have sealed itself shut. Nevertheless, she'll need blood to heal the damage you've done. You won't have to worry about finding her again; she'll seek you out to settle what you started."

It began to rain, an icy slicing sleet that forced both men to pull their cloaks closer. Markus looked up at the flash of lightning that set the sky ablaze in violent shades of blue and purple. "There's something unnatural about that storm."

"I doubt it originated in nature. I believe Bathory conjured this up to slow us down."

Before Markus could reply there came a shout, and the voices of other soldiers followed. A band of Spielsdorf's men approached, half carrying/half dragging a girl behind them. As they drew closer, Markus was surprised at the resemblance between this girl and Carmilla. A flash of silver in the moonlight revealed a crucifix hung from a necklace about her neck, placed there by one of the soldiers to restrict her vampiric abilities.

General Spielsdorf looked at the officer in charge of the group, Major Arcana, who sported a black leather patch over the socket where his left eye had once been. There was no need to even voice the question. Stepping forward, Arcana shook his head. "Countess Bathory escaped, but we managed to capture this one."

Gripping the girl by the chin, Spielsdorf lifted her face up toward his. "Good evening, Elga."

"Finish it" was her only response.

Arcana glanced at Elga. "She's not afraid to die…not like the others."

Spielsdorf nodded. "It was her willingness to embrace death that made her the creature that she is."

Markus raised one of the Kukri knives and prepared to strike Elga's head from her shoulders, but Spielsdorf held up a restraining hand. "No, not yet." The general turned away and began to walk back toward his horse. "Bring her along; perhaps we can use her as bait to lure her companions out of hiding."

*

Lightning shredded the dark horizon, skeletal electric fingers that tore at the clouds to allow even more water to pour out onto the earth. Sandor dug his heels into his horse's ribs and buried his face in its mane to keep the stinging rain out of his eyes. Spurring the animal did little good; it could not be forced into more than a trot, yet Sandor could find no fault with the beast. The horse was as exhausted as he was. The sky had seemed so clear when rider and mount had set out that afternoon. If it had not been for the weather, they could have made Buda-Pest by morning. With little hope of that now, Sandor's only goal was to find shelter for the night.

Again the darkness exploded white with lightning, and the deafening crack of thunder caused the horse to stop short and dig at the ground with its front hooves. The whole beast's body trembled from terror and cold as its eyes flashed about, disturbed by something unseen yet still sensed. Sandor squinted ahead in the grainy darkness. In that brief instant the lightning had blasted the night it seemed as if a human form hovered over the crossroads before him, a pale figure floating in mid-air beneath the tall trees that arched over the path. Sandor shook his head to fling the wet, serpentine locks of hair out of his face. The lightning was playing tricks on him; if not on his nerves, then certainly on his eyes. He urged his shivering mount onward, patting its neck and speaking gently to calm the poor animal. "I don't know if you're more frozen or scared; either way, staying here won't help."

As horse and rider neared the point where the roads crossed, man and beast strained to see into the gloom for something that both knew should not be there. Suddenly the horse burst into a gallop, crashing ahead as if to dash past the imagined danger, its hooves sending clods of thick wet mud flying out into the night. They had just reached the crossing when the storm blew out one of the two riding lanterns hanging from the stirrups. Wrenching at the reins and swearing under his breath, Sandor brought the horse to a halt and swung himself down. If he were lucky, he thought, he would be able to re-light the extinguished lamp from the one still burning. The man’s mouth twitched into a sardonic smile as it occurred to him that if he really were lucky, both would still be ablaze.

Hardly had Sandor unhooked the darkened lantern when he heard a faint creaking, like the sound of moist hemp being wound tight. Although he could see nothing, he sensed something swaying in the wind directly overhead. Lightning again bathed the landscape and, as the nightmarish scene the blue/white light revealed was plunged back into darkness, the lantern went crashing from Sandor's hands to the ground. There *was* a body suspended from one of the trees, hanging just above him. The wet rope groaned beneath the weight as it swung back and forth, blown about by the gusts of wind that swept through the nocturnal world.

Sandor crossed himself. Probably the corpse of an executed criminal, some highwayman or murderer hung there as an object lesson for all to see. No sooner had this thought passed through his mind when another dazzling burst of electricity reached across the heavens, but this time the Promethean fire seemed unnaturally prolonged, leaving a more vivid image burnt into Sandor's memory. This was no corpse, nor highwayman. The wet, white shroud clung like a glistening membrane to the young woman's body, the rain rendering the filmy cloth almost invisible. The electrical illumination, so intense that her garment glowed, had lasted long enough for him to see she did not hang by the neck, but had been bound from foot to shoulder, and suspended above the road by a rope running from the tree and tied carefully beneath her arms in such a way as to keep her alive. Just before the light faded, the body had turned and her eyes met his.

A violent shudder passed through Sandor. What was this unfortunate girl's crime that she had been left like this on such a night? He took the remaining lantern from the stirrups of his saddle and held it up, ignoring the horse as it snorted and pawed at the ground. The rope holding the girl was stretched over a branch and tied off at a signpost marking the crossroads. Her eyes glistened in the faint lamplight, silently pleading with him. Sandor's attention was so focused on his discovery that he was unaware of the other two pairs of eyes fixed upon him with equal intensity.

Hidden behind the mass of tangled undergrowth and wild bushes along the roadside, eyes filled with hatred and hunger glared at the traveler from the window of an elegant ebony carriage. The intricate woodwork of the coach was accented by the darkened gilded lamps, and engraved beneath the rear window was the letter "B" in an oval inlaid with gold. On either door of the vehicle was a crest depicting three wolf teeth beneath a crown, encircled by a dragon biting its tail: The seal of the House of Bathory.

The interior was as luxurious as the exterior, with deep seats, cushioned lining, and heavy window drapes of leather, satin, and velvet done in soft greys and blues. Two women wrapped in dark cloaks occupied the carriage. The owner, Countess Bathory, watched her young companion almost as closely as she watched Sandor. Carmilla's recklessness had caused problems in the past. It was because of her that they had been forced to flee their homeland, and earlier that night she had nearly gotten them...Bathory smiled to herself as she realized she was about to use the word "killed." There was something feral about her heart-shaped mouth as the wet ruby lips parted to reveal pearly teeth. Beneath the shadows of her hooded cape Bathory's sapphire eyes glistened with amusement, as if lit by some inner fire. The humor quickly passed as she recalled the circumstances that had brought them to this desolate spot and anger again filled her.

"Why doesn't he help her?" Carmilla's whisper was almost a hiss, the glow in her dark eyes reflecting her rage. "He needs a lesson in chivalry."

Bathory threw back the hood of her cloak, letting a golden cascade of curls pour down over her shoulders and flow to her waist as she leaned towards the window. Her attention was no longer divided, but now focused only on the crossroads. "We can do nothing until he takes the first step; General Spielsdorf has seen to that. At least we were able to use the weather to drive his soldiers away."

At the mention of the general's name, Carmilla slipped one hand beneath her cloak to touch the bare flesh of her left shoulder. She had glutted herself on enough blood to restore her youth, but the wound from the silver-plated blade had still not completely healed. Outside, the roar of thunder seemed to echo her frustration.

Beneath the hangman's tree came a soft faint voice barely loud enough to be heard above nature's revelry as it reached Sandor's ears. "Help me." Or had he heard it? It seemed more like a thought than a sound.

Taking the hunting knife he kept sheathed inside one boot, Sandor carefully cut the rope where it was tied to the signpost, his gloved hands gripping the wet cord tightly to keep the girl from plunging to the ground. Slowly he lowered her, his arms aching from the cold and strain. The moment her body touched the earth, his horse cried out in terror and bolted off into the night. Sandor began to dash after the fleeing animal when again came the weak whispered plea, "Help me." This time there was no mistaking that he had actually heard a voice.

Returning his knife to the boot sheath, Sandor turned back to the girl, silently praying the horse would return. At least the rain was lessening. As he knelt down beside the girl, he placed the lantern by her head. The ordeal must have taken its toll on her, as she made no attempt to struggle against her bonds.

Seeing her cousin lowered from the makeshift gallows, Carmilla stepped silently from the coach, only to be held back by Bathory and found herself wincing at the firm grip. In her weakened state, she was unable to shrug off the restraining hand.

"No, not yet; not until he has released her." Bathory realized the girl was in pain and relaxed her grasp, patting her gently on the shoulder. "Patience, Carmilla, patience."

Beneath the older woman's apparent calm, Carmilla could sense the suppressed sadness. "Yes, Aunt Elizabeth."

Sandor tore off his gloves and began to untie the shivering body before him, her flesh feverish in spite of the night. He halted for a moment, puzzled by a strange sight; entwined in the ropes were cloves of garlic. She wore a crown of thorns upon her head, and a small silver crucifix and chain hung around her soft white throat. His hands were nearly numb from the cold as his trembling fingers tugged painfully at the taut, wet knots. "What's your name?"

"Elga."

“I’m Sandor, Erich Sandor.” As he worked the last knots free, the clouds overhead pulled away to reveal the autumn moon. "At least the weather's clearing off," Sandor said, trying to raise her spirits.

"Will you take the cross and chain off? The metal is cold, and my hands and fingers are too stiff for me to use."

Gently he raised Elga up and carefully removed the crown of thorns. In the dim light, Sandor could not see the punctures made by the barbs slowly begin to heal. Removing the crucifix that encircled her neck, he suddenly remembered her near-nakedness. He slipped off his cloak and placed it about her. "Here; it's wet, but it's bound to be warmer than what you were left with."

Elga looked at him, her eyes filled with pity. There had been no sound before the two unseen observers were on him, teeth flashing and gnashing in the lamp fire as they tore at him like starving wolves with a piece of meat. Their taloned hands ripped through his clothes and skin, pulling him down as their mouths locked onto exposed flesh, and he could hear the sounds of their tongues and lips lapping and sucking at the fresh wounds.

As Sandor was thrown back onto the lantern, shattering it and extinguishing the flame, his hand went to the weapon in his boot. Hardly had he drawn it when Elga wrenched it from him, her eyes blazing in the dark at the sight of the man's blood. He cried out, his breath and blood steaming in the cold night air. Elga's teeth clamped down on his throat, crushing it until his screams became a mere gurgle. The knife landed several feet away in the mud, the rain glistening on the blade like drops of silver beneath the moon.

*

The icy steel blades of the sabers glistened like frozen silver, and the muted colors of the softly lit corridor formed an odd contrast with the harsh sounds of slashing steel. Abraham "Bram" Van Helsing, his pants and shirt stained with sweat and dirt, swung his sword up to block the blade of his opponent, Gerald Wellington, who was precariously perched atop the mantelpiece of the mammoth fireplace that dominated the great hall. Grimacing, Van Helsing deflected the oncoming blade to his right while his gloved left hand shot upward, grasping his sparring partner by the throat and dragging him down from the ledge. Van Helsing doubled over as Wellington's boot caught him in the stomach and both men went crashing in a heap onto the floor.

Van Helsing sprang up and used the hilt of his sword to strike at Wellington's head. Just as the oncoming pommel was about to crush his temple, Wellington caught the hilt with his left hand and rammed the hilt of his own weapon in Van Helsing's groin.

Wellington quickly sprang back, vanishing into the shadows as a gasping Van Helsing lunged at him, only to slip and land face down on the ancient marble floor. Panting heavily, Van Helsing clutched at his stomach and rolled onto his side. The cool stone against his feverish face was a relief, momentarily taking his mind away from the dull pain that hammered away at him. Where was his opponent? Hearing footsteps echo a short distance away, he took a deep breath, winced, and forced himself to his feet.

Van Helsing limped down the corridor until he reached the end, which opened on a magnificent ballroom ruled over by an enormous crystal chandelier. The chamber, lit only with the cold morning light that struggled in through the long stained-glass windows at either end, radiated a somber feeling of foreboding. Except for the dim twinkle of light reflected off the chandelier, the entire room was absent of any movement. Staggering to a group of pillars at the far end of the ballroom, Van Helsing leaned against one of the columns, exhausted. His brown hair clung to his moist forehead and sweat trickled into his eyes, burning them as he strained to see in the gloom. From somewhere in the shadow-filled chamber came a sharp crunching sound. Van Helsing sprang away from the pillar, spinning around and holding his sword at the ready. Hoping to lure his foe into a shaft of colored light, he backed away from his resting place and slowly made his way towards one of the windows.

From Van Helsing's left came a flash of steel. With a premature cry of triumph Wellington charged Van Helsing, who nimbly sidestepped him while delivering a swift passing kick to the fellow's backside. Wellington immediately recovered and whirled about, only to be disarmed with a quick twist of Van Helsing's sword. Pushing the point of his blade firmly into the fleshy underside of Wellington's chin, Van Helsing forced the defeated man against a window, where the light from the colored glass had a prismatic effect on his blond hair. Van Helsing pressed the sword more firmly into the fellow, whose efforts to slip free pushed open the window. Teetering on the ledge, Wellington glanced nervously over one shoulder at the drop behind him.

An authoritative voice resonated throughout the ballroom: "We do not practice the saber in the halls and ballroom! Van Helsing, get your roommate out of the window."

Tossing his sword aside, Van Helsing pulled Wellington back into the room as the elderly newcomer approached them. Wellington rested a hand on Van Helsing's shoulder, giving the older man a weary grin before gasping a greeting. "Good morning, Dr. Belasko. I hope my associate here turns to a more delicate instrument once he becomes a surgeon."

"*If* he becomes a surgeon," Belasko corrected, shaking his head. "Perhaps if the two of you would apply your minds as energetically as you do your bodies...?" The professor's moist grey eyes glinted behind his spectacles as he sized the two students up. For the first time since arriving at the university, Van Helsing realized those eyes were identical to the salt-and-pepper color of the doctor's hair, and wondered if they had always been a matched set. Further speculation was cut off as Belasko added, "Look at you; your clothes tattered and torn like a couple of orphans. I'd hate to see the bill from your tailor...or is that yet another service the ladies provide?"

"Ladies?" Wellington asked, feigning ignorance. "What ladies?"

"Gerald knows a lot of girls," Van Helsing called over one shoulder as he retrieved his sword, "but I'm not sure many, if any, qualify for 'lady' status."

"Regardless of their social position," Belasko said, "I am aware you two are not unfamiliar with an establishment known as the Wolf's Head, and that Master Wellington here has been keeping company with one of the tavern wenches. Being a firm believer in poetic justice, I can only say that it gives me great pleasure to know that the day will come when you shall have children of your own to contend with."

“How does he know that day hasn’t already come?” Van Helsing murmured beneath his breath to Wellington, only to find Belasko had overheard the remark. He felt his face go flush beneath the elderly academic’s withering gaze.

"Spare me your wit until you have learned to hone it as sharp as your blade,” Belasko advised. “Many here in Buda-Pest feel the university has a heritage to be proud of, although that may come as a surprise to the two of you. You’ve been shown a great deal of tolerance because you both show remarkable academic promise, but I needn't tell you the anatomy master was not impressed by the incident in the surgical theatre last week. I warned you then that I would be forced to place you on probation for the duration of the term. It may interest you to know that I've just come from your rooms."

The two students exchanged wary glances.

"I was amazed to find, among other things, a rather unusual smoking apparatus," the professor continued, "made from various glassware smuggled out of the chemistry department."

"‘Once more unto the breach,’" Van Helsing sighed. “Are we to be suspended again?”

"You put me in a difficult position, Van Helsing" Belasko replied gravely. "However, I am inclined to give you one final chance. I would be willing to overlook the offense if you were to dismantle the device and return its components back to the laboratory."

"Consider it done!" Wellington promised, stepping forward to shake Belasko's hand. He stopped in mid-step at the professor's icy stare, and his sudden enthusiasm vanished.

"And," Belasko added, taking silent pride in the electrifying effect that one little word had on them, "if you can procure a specimen for the anatomy class for use in the dissection demonstration the day after tomorrow."

"A human specimen?" Wellington asked.

"Of course a human! You can't expect to become a surgeon by chopping up chickens."

Van Helsing could not believe his ears. It had been a bit of body snatching gone wrong that had gotten them expelled from Edinburgh. "But the only corpses we're allowed to experiment on are executed criminals from the prison. You *want* us to break the law?"

"It is an area for which the two of you show a decided talent. Dissection has been almost impossible this year because of a shortage from the gallows. That's the trouble with the judicial system these days; they are far too lenient with the riff-raff roaming the streets. And I dare say that will be your fate, if you don't start exercising a little more self-discipline." Making sure no one could see or overhear, Belasko reached into his jacket and took out a slender brown slip of paper. “Perhaps this will make matters a little easier for you,” he said, handing the paper to Wellington. “You will wait until you are outside before reading it, and then you will destroy it.”

After the students’ footsteps faded away and Belasko found himself alone, he cleaned off the lenses of his glasses with his handkerchief and then carefully placed the spectacles in his breast pocket. Looking about the murky room to make sure he had no audience, with a hissed "*En garde!*” the professor lunged at an imaginary opponent with an equally imaginary sword. He cringed at the instant twinge in his back. “Oh, to be young again….”

Van Helsing and Wellington made their way slowly down the steps of the university's main hall, draping their cloaks over their shoulders as they crossed the brick walkway, and stepped out into the wet cobblestone street. As Wellington adjusted the collar of his coat, he thought aloud, "I wonder where we’ll be expelled from next? Maybe we should try London; I have family there, you know."

“And an ex-fiancée,” Van Helsing pointed out before taking a deep breath of crisp autumn air and slowly letting it out with a contented sigh. “Her father wouldn’t mind doing a bit of dissecting on you.”

Avoiding Van Helsing’s gaze, Wellington looked about at the small shops across the square, where a group of apprentices were busy sweeping off the walks in front of their masters' offices. “She’s married now, so that danger should be over.”

“Much like our careers here if we don’t come up with a body. By the time we finally finish university, we’ll be old enough to retire. Where are we going to get a corpse on such short notice? The weather’s too raw to be mucking about in the churchyard at night."

“Let’s see what this is all about.” Wellington opened the note Belasko had given him. His mouth slowly curved into a smile as he silently read the contents. “I believe Lady Luck is about to embrace us.”

"The last time you said that, we were the overnight guests of the local magistrate. You'll recall his accommodations did not include bed and breakfast."

“Don’t be such a pessimist. You’ll be pleased to know we won’t have to do any digging in the graveyard. According to Belasko’s note, a body was brought to the morgue yesterday morning.”

“It isn’t anyone we know, is it?” Van Helsing asked. “Remember what happened in Scotland…?”

"I’ve never heard of him; a local merchant named Sandor, killed on the road from Klausenburg. All we have to do is slip ourselves in, and then slip him out. All in all, a rather uneventful evening."

Van Helsing smiled. “I look forward to being blissfully bored.”

Wellington gave the note a last look before crumpling it in his fist. “Hopefully the body’s not too tattered; apparently he was attacked by some sort of animal.”

2. A Grim Undertaking.

As the clock tower rang out the hour of midnight, the slow but steady hiss of sleet against the window of the morgue office showed no promise of letting up. Hunyadi, the morgue's night attendant, had fallen asleep in the chair at his desk but awoke at the sound of the tower bells and shivered. The room had grown cooler since his last bout of consciousness. Reluctantly pushing himself to a standing position, the pot-bellied man stretched his limbs, his cherry-red face wincing at the popping and cracking of his seldom-used joints. Walking stiffly to the heavy wooden door that opened onto the cobblestone street, he drew back the bolt and swung it open, then took a deep breath so that the rush of cold air into his lungs would reawaken his senses. An approaching carriage could be heard in the distance, and Hunyadi looked down the darkened street toward the source of the sound.

The clopping of hoofbeats and metallic rattle of wheel rims on the rain-swept stones were accompanied by a gust of wind, and the unseen carriage came into view as it turned onto the street. At first glance it appeared to be more shadow than substance, for the coach and four-horse team were all black, and no light came from the windows or lamps. As it passed by, the gold fixtures and the crest on the carriage door glistened in the light spilling out from around Hunyadi as he stood in the morgue doorway. A pair of brilliant blue eyes glared mockingly from deep within the carriage interior. The night quickly swallowed the carriage, giving only a brief glimpse of the ornate letter "B" beneath the rear window before the vehicle vanished.

The sleet increased in intensity and Hunyadi quickly shut the door, bolting it behind him. His eyes came to rest on the double doors on the opposite end of the office, which lead to the holding room. He frowned at the sounds of squeaking and scratching that came from the other side. With slightly trembling hands, a side effect of drink as much as fear, he took a lamp from its bracket in the wall and armed himself with the poker from the fireplace. As he slowly crept to the doors, the scraping noise growing louder with each step.

Reaching his destination, Hunyadi found it almost impossible to twist the key in the ancient iron lock. Why it was necessary to keep the room locked remained a mystery to the attendant; the bodies inside were not likely to wander off. Sitting the lamp and poker aside, Hunyadi used both hands to turn the key. Suddenly the lock shot open with a sharp metallic crack, and the scratching on the opposite side of the doors stopped. Snatching up the poker and light, the attendant made the sign of the cross with the lamp and threw open the door. Silence greeted him as he peered into the darkened room, occupied only by the shrouded forms laid out upon the oblong tables.

"Hell," he muttered to himself, "I wouldn't send the likes of any of you out on a night like this." Again came the tiny screeching sounds. The morgue attendant stepped back, gasping as a plump mouse scattered playfully across his shoes and up the side of his leg. "Nor you, either, friend, even if you did add a few grey hairs to my head just now." The man laughed, picking the mouse up by its tail. The bloated ball of fur chattered its annoyance at such indelicate treatment.

Across the street from the morgue, Van Helsing and Wellington huddled in a doorway in vain hopes the wintry weather would lessen. Sticking one hand out into the downpour, Wellington quickly yanked it back. "I think it's getting colder; this could turn to snow soon."

"I wish we were back in Edinburgh," Van Helsing muttered. "If it hadn't been for that business with Burke and Hare in Surgeon's Square…."

"Let that be a lesson to you," Wellington said. "Sloth never pays off. If Burke and Hare had stuck to robbing graves to supply the classrooms with cadavers instead of simply murdering streetwalkers, there wouldn't have been angry mobs attacking instructors and students alike. You'd think *we* were the body snatchers."

"At times we were," Van Helsing reminded him. "Remember?"

"I remember Mary, with those gorgeous red curls and dark eyes."

Van Helsing looked at him with a mixture of amazement and amusement. "You mean Mary Patterson, the prostitute? Are you getting nostalgic over a tart?"

"Not all anatomy is academic. Besides, she wasn't like the others; I was very fond of her."

"So were a lot of the lads in Edinburgh. She was a particular favorite among Dr. Knox's students…."

"And how would you know that?" Wellington asked, suddenly uncomfortable with the conversation. "Considering your celibacy, perhaps priest would be more suitable than surgeon."

Van Helsing ignored the intended insult, "I'm sorry Burke and Hare got to her; I was just as shocked as you when she showed up on the dissection table. There wasn't a student in that lecture hall that wouldn't have literally skinned those two alive for what they'd done. But you've got Gretchen now.

"Unlike you and Christine, Gretchen is not a long-term relationship. Can you see the look on father's face if I brought home a barmaid?"

"As opposed to you bringing home someone like Mary?"

"Back then, I didn't plan on going back home. After graduation I would have stayed on in Edinburgh." Wellington smiled, but there was no humor in his eyes. "Dr. Knox had offered me a position as his assistant. Needless to say, his association with Burke and Hare brought all that to an end."

"Gretchen does love you, you know."

"Look, this isn't some romantic faerie tale where everything is in black & white and everyone lives happily ever after," Wellington snapped. "This is the real world where things are grey and dirty. Gretchen is a chapter of my life, not the whole bloody book."

"Keep your voice down," Van Helsing hissed. "Forget I mentioned it. Let's just get the body and take it back to the university so Vambery can get it ready for the lecture."

"Fine." Wellington dug into the pocket of his cloak and came out with a handful of grey hair. "Here, put these on."

"What is it?"

"Your wig and moustache."

Van Helsing was sure he had heard wrong. "What?"

"Your wig and moustache. Put it on; you look too young to be an official. They don't just hand out bodies to anyone who comes knocking at their door."

With the mouse now housed in his shirt pocket, Hunyadi jabbed at the glowing embers of the fireplace with a poker in an effort to warm the morgue office. He picked up the pewter pot of rum he had left to simmer on the hearth, the metal handle carefully wrapped in cloth to guard against burns, and gratefully sniffed at the hot brew as he filled the tankard on his desk. Poking its head out of the pocket, the mouse twitched its nose at the aroma wafting up from the tankard.

"Think you'd like a taste of this?" Hunyadi asked, slipping back into his chair. He took a cautious sip of the dark, steaming grog, feeling it flow down his throat as an inner warmth rose up from within to drive the chill from his spine. Carefully removing his new friend from his pocket, he dangled the mouse by its tail over the stein. The mouse sniffed curiously at the rum before deciding to try it. As Hunyadi slowly lowered the mouse down to the tankard for a sip, a sharp series of knocks sounded at the outer door. The startled man leaped to his feet, dropping the mouse into the rum.

On the morgue doorstep, Wellington gave Van Helsing's appearance a final check. The rain was causing his disguise to droop on one side. Hearing the sounds of the door's bolt being thrown back, Wellington shoved his companion out of sight and said, "Give me five minutes."

"Right."

"And fix your moustache!"

Hunyadi opened the door, mumbling and grumbling about the interruption beneath his breath. Visits at such an hour were few and far between, and usually meant a new arrival. As a result, it was surprising for the attendant to find a young man with a look of self-importance about him standing on the step, his hat cocked to one side and his cape billowing in the breeze.

"Hunyadi?" Wellington asked.

"Yes?"

"Wilhelm Hunyadi?"

"That would be me, sir; I'm the night attendant."

"Good," beamed the drenched figure, stepping inside and removing his hat. "I wanted to be sure I had the man in charge." Hunyadi's eyes glowed with pride and drink as the newcomer continued, "My name is Gerald Wellington, newly appointed Master-at-Arms to the Royal Medical Society. You have here, I believe, the body of one Erich Sandor?"

"Sounds familiar." Hunyadi shut the door and then went to his desk to consult the logbook. "Here he is; came in two mornings ago. A nasty business; looks like the work of a wolf."

"Excellent. Would you be so kind as to double-check? I want to be sure I have the right fellow." There was a touch of pleading to Wellington's smile and tone. He added confidentially, "I'm glad we'll be working with a man of your experience in such an urgent matter, especially given the delicacy and discretion of the case."

Hunyadi almost bowed, but decided restraint would be more in order and was content merely to nod his head with a knowing wink. The attendant excused himself and once more took his lamp down from the wall, going to the holding room to find the body in question.

Alone in the office, Wellington dropped his cool exterior and looked nervously about the dingy room. He could feel, even hear, his heart pounding against his chest. Then the smell of rum reached his nose and his attention fell upon the steaming tankard on the desk. Moving quickly, before the attendant could come back, Wellington snatched up the stein and drank it down, only to find himself with a mouthful of mouse. Gagging, he spat the contents back into the mug, the mouse screeching and scolding the student. He had barely put the tankard back on the desk when Hunyadi returned.

"He's here, sir, just as we thought," the attendant confirmed. "Apparently bled to death from wounds received in the attack."

"You're sure it was a wolf?" Wellington asked, mustering every once of sobriety he possessed. He could still feel moist mouse hair on his tongue.

"Yes, sir. At least that's what was written on his chart. Says they even found and killed such a beast."

"How old was he?"

"The wolf?"

"The man," sighed Wellington, "how old was the man?"

"Thirty-four, according to the report." Hunyadi's eyes narrowed with suspicion. "What's going on here?"

"Dr. Van Helsing will explain everything. He should be arriving any moment." On the pretext of consulting his pocket watch, Wellington turned away from Hunyadi so that the attendant could not see him scrape his tongue through his teeth to get rid of the fuzzy feeling. The sudden rap-tap-tapping of a walking stick against the outer door of the office caused both men to jump, with Wellington nearly biting the tip of his tongue off in the process.

"'Quiet as a morgue,' indeed" Hunyadi muttered as he went to unlatch the door. "I'll never get any sleep at this rate." Barely had he opened the door when a man in black swept into the room from the downpour. Handing Hunyadi his cane and Wellington his small leather medical case, the commanding figure proceeded to brush the water off his hat. The morgue attendant looked curiously at this second visitor. With his shock of wild grey hair and massive whiskers that ran down either side of his face and met under his nose, he looked almost rabid. Hunyadi was almost afraid to venture the question. "Dr. Van Helsing?"

"I am Van Helsing," the man responded with a prim smile, handing the bewildered attendant his hat. His hands free, the "elderly" doctor removed his pair of pince-nez and wiped the rain from their lenses. Replacing the tiny spectacles upon the end of his nose, Van Helsing turned to Wellington and asked hesitantly, "Is he...?"

"Yes, doctor, in the next room," Wellington responded with professional curtness. Nodding toward Hunyadi, he added, "He claims the man is the victim of a wolf."

"That's what they put on the paper," piped up the attendant, fearing he might be blamed for a serious clerical error.

"We must lose no more time," Van Helsing insisted. "Herr Hunyadi, if you will be good enough to show us the body of Herr Sandor."

Hunyadi handed Wellington the lamp he had been holding and fetched a second one for himself. Once more the attendant opened the double doors to the holding room and led the way in. The shadows that danced in the lamplight threatened to close in and smother the three men and their spluttering flames. Above the deep rumble of thunder, Van Helsing asked, "Which one is he?"

"There on the end," Hunyadi responded, lifting his lamp to push the darkness back from them.

Van Helsing and Wellington stepped toward the designated table. As they drew closer, Van Helsing raised a cautioning hand and his companion held back. Hunyadi, who was more than content to stand even further away, felt his chest tighten as Van Helsing gripped the sheet covering the corpse and whipped it away with grim determination. Van Helsing looked back over one shoulder, his eyes wide with disbelief, and Hunyadi felt his heart surge up into his throat.

"The lamp," Van Helsing demanded in firm, commanding tones that did little to ease the attendant's nerves. Wellington approached the body and placed his lamp next to the corpse's head to provide a better view. It was all either of them could do to carry on the charade, and they shuddered at the shock of the sight. Sandor's throat had been badly savaged, and there were scattered wounds covering the chest and wrists. There was no doubt that it was the work of very sharp teeth; such deep punctures could have only been made from an animal's fangs.

Van Helsing bent over the dead man, removing his gloves as he did so, and began to examine the wounds. "Gott in Himmel!" he hissed, slipping into his native tongue as he often did when excited or thinking aloud. Slowly he looked up at Wellington, his eyes filled with disbelief as he whispered, "The fellow's been *gnawed*."

"The report said a wolf was killed in the area after this. It could have been the same animal"

"But there's no blood. And what animal has a jaw span this size? Look at the arrangement of marks left by the teeth. These bites were made by a human!"

Wellington recalled reports of cannibalism on tropical islands made by returning sailors, and tried to put the thought out of his head. "Look, let's just get through this and get out of here," he urged quietly. In a voice loud enough for Hunyadi to hear, he asked "Was it a wild animal, or...?" Wellington let his voice trail off for dramatic effect.

"No," Van Helsing shook his head and crossed himself. Looking up at Wellington, his face was a mask of grim determination. "This is no normal wolf; we're looking at an outbreak of *Mariphasa lupina lumina*."

"What is it?" Hunyadi asked, his curiosity battling a rising sense of dread for dominance.

"Those marks on the throat," Wellington's voice was theatrically hesitant. "Are you familiar with a condition called lycanthropy? A werewolf may be at work here. Have you ever seen these types of wounds on any of the other bodies brought in, especially within the last two weeks?" Wellington stepped back as Hunyadi came closer for a better look at the wounds.

With a reassuring smile to Hunyadi, Van Helsing held out one hand toward Wellington. "I'll need my instrument case." Wellington handed him the case, which Van Helsing placed on the edge of the table next to Sandor's head. He gently opened the case before swiftly whirling to deliver a sharp uppercut to the chin of the morgue attendant, who collapsed unconscious into Wellington's waiting arms.

The two students lifted the unfortunate fellow onto a nearby slab and covered him with a sheet. Still moving quickly, Van Helsing peeled off his fake whiskers and grey wig while Wellington produced a large canvas bag that had been hidden beneath his cloak. The whiskers, along with the prop spectacles and wig, were crammed into the medical case.

"We don't get many like this," Wellington remarked, like a connoisseur sampling a rare vintage. "It's so fresh. Too bad about the throat and chest, though."

"What about that right wrist? That's no small bite."

"I just hope there's no severe internal damage done. Do you know how long it's been since we've been able to examine healthy organs?"

"Let's hope this donation to the dissection room gets Dr. Belasko off our backs for a bit." Wellington began guiding the canvas sack around the Sandor's feet and ankles, and then worked it up around the legs. "We've missed too many lectures and just about lost our bargaining power," he puffed, trying to cram the head and shoulders down into the bag. "Give me a hand with this, will you?" Hardly were the words out of his mouth when Wellington jumped away from the table, letting corpse and canvas crash to the floor. "His neck," he screeched. "Look at his neck!"

Van Helsing knelt by the body, and his eyes narrowed. It must be the shadows, playing tricks on him. Grabbing at the lamp on the table beside him, he held the flickering light close to the corpse. "The wounds on his throat…they're gone."

"It's like he was never touched."

Both men let out a cry as the body on the table next to them sat up, its head still draped with a dingy sheet. Realizing it was Hunyadi, Van Helsing struck him again. With a muffled moan, the attendant fell back onto the table.

"Let's have a look at that wrist." Van Helsing reached into the bag and lifted Sandor's right arm up. Before his disbelieving eyes, the wounds were slowly closing and healing.

Wellington stuffed the arm back down into the bag. "I don't know what's going on here, but let's get this thing back to the university and be done with it."

"Maybe we should just leave it."

"If we do that, we end up leaving the university."

The shock of the night air and the openness of the streets were a refreshing relief after the claustrophobic confines of the morgue. The bricks and stones glistened oily black about them as Van Helsing and Wellington hauled their prize to the waiting horse cart.

Gathering itself out of the blackness of the shadows, far enough away to go unnoticed by the two students, came the dark coach and team of horses. Inside, three women watched with cat-like curiosity as the canvas-covered corpse was placed into the cart and tied down. Anyone casting a casual glance inside the coach would have thought the girls were returning from a ball, as all wore ornate dresses of identical design, with Bathory in blue, Carmilla in crimson and Elga in emerald green. Moving forward in her seat to get a better look at the young men, Carmilla unconsciously ran her tongue along the inside of her teeth as she thought of their blood gushing over her cool lips, warming them.

"Not too close," Countess Bathory cautioned, a warning hand placed on the girl's forearm. "Watch and wait before we make ourselves known."

"Yes, Aunt Elizabeth," came the impatient sigh.

Elga slipped alongside Carmilla, who was still gazing intently out the window. "Why, they're taking a body *from* the morgue."

A gleeful glint in her eye, Carmilla pressed her face to Elga's and spoke in conspiratorial tones. "You don't think they'll do anything strange with it, do you?"

Bathory shook her head, her hair rustling in the silence. "After all these years, Carmilla, you still haven't learned restraint. Is that really all your mind can find to amuse itself?"

"She's always been that way, even when she was alive. Nothing ever satisfies her unless it's scandalous."

Carmilla shrugged. "Is it my fault I'm restless?"

Elga arched a disapproving eyebrow. "Don't go on again about how bored you are. Sometimes I think you would have died of boredom if you hadn't...."

"Better to have died from living too much than too little. I may have often been bored but at least *I* was never boring, was I?" Carmilla ran her fingers caressingly through her cousin's hair. Elga knocked the teasing hand away, hissing as her lips pulled back to reveal the long, lustrous teeth. Carmilla laughed. "So, pretty pussy learns it has claws. Come, kitten; let us kiss and make up."

As quickly as it came Elga's fury passed. Sulking, she said, "You shouldn't have come with us tonight. You haven't completely recovered from the General's attack."

"All the more reason to be out hunting."

"You need rest."

"Oh, you *do* care about me. My little cousin is going to become my personal physician."

Elga glared at her. "What you need is a good leeching."

"Be still, both of you!" Bathory hissed. Her pale blue eyes glowed with an inner light as she watched Van Helsing and Gerald set off in the cart. "The body they've taken is the one we came for."

"The fellow we feasted on?" asked Carmilla. "Is that why we're here, so you can revive him?"

"Yes," Bathory said. "I want to use him as a decoy to draw Spielsdorf out into the open, the way the general tried to use Elga to trap us." Opening the carriage window, the countess called out to the driver, "Follow them, but stay out of sight. I want to see where they go and what they know."

The coach lurched into pursuit as Elga asked, "What would they want with him?"

Carmilla's mouth curved into a wicked smile, the expression mirrored in her eyes. "I know what he'll want with *them*."

Leaning forward, as if to shorten the distance between herself and Sandor, Bathory closed her eyes and began to concentrate. "If I can go into his thoughts and make his mind one with mine...."

As Wellington guided the open cart through the alleys and side streets, Bram looked back at the shrouded form behind the seat and pulled his cloak tighter about him. "You could have at least stolen a hearse."

"We were lucky to get this. Besides, a hearse on the road at this hour might be a little conspicuous."

Van Helsing again glanced toward the back of the vehicle, straining his eyes and ears. The darkened streets were deserted.

"What is it?" Wellington asked.

"I could have sworn I heard a coach and horses following us."

"Probably just the echo of our own rig. You're not going to lose your nerve on me after all these years, are you?"

"Why should I lose my nerve now?" laughed Van Helsing. "Can things get worse?"

A cold, claw-like hand clamped over Van Helsing's face and yanked him into the back of the cart. His head cracked against the wooden floor and he lay in a daze, stunned as much from the blow as from the sight that greeted him. Sandor, or at least what had once been Sandor, towered over the student. The flesh was ghastly pale, and the red-rimmed eyes glowed as they gloated at Van Helsing. The dark lips were a crimson-gashed mockery of a mouth that pulled back to reveal the cruel canine teeth, elongated ivory spikes glistening with saliva.

3. The Quick and the Dead.

"Mein Gott," Van Helsing whispered, crossing himself at the sight of the newborn vampire standing over him. Wellington, never releasing the reins, glanced over one shoulder at the sight and crossed himself as well.

In her carriage, still following the two medical students at a distance, Elizabeth Bathory was oblivious to her two nieces. Although her eyes had rolled up until only the whites showed, she could still see Abraham Van Helsing and Gerald Wellington through the eyes of the reborn Sandor. "He's alive," she whispered.

The reins fell from Wellington's hands as his mouth fell open in terror. "It's alive!"

"I can see that," Van Helsing managed.

As Van Helsing scurried to the far corner of the cart, Sandor could smell the young man's fear and hear his heart racing as rapidly as the wagon itself. The vampire's tongue licked at his lips as he thought of how the blood would spurt from the punctured flesh. The throat looked like it would yield easily enough.

A sharp crack sounded in Sandor's ear, and the vampire's own throat suddenly seemed ablaze beneath the sharp stroke of a leather lash. Wellington had snatched up the horsewhip and was slashing away at Sandor with the makeshift weapon. The vampire caught the whip in one hand, yanking on it to hurl Wellington headlong into the back with Van Helsing. The driverless cart careened around a corner, sending the two friends tumbling about in the back.

"A two-course meal," Sandor chuckled, tossing the whip aside as the welts from the whip healed. Stepping closer, he continued, "And such tender young hens, plump and ready for plucking." The vampire focused his attention on Wellington, sniffing the air like a hound picking up the scent of its prey. His eyes filled with hunger as he knelt over the student and whispered, "Fee, Fi, Fo, Fum, I smell the blood of an Englishman."

A staccato sound shuddered throughout the vehicle as the horse ran too close to a stretch of wrought iron fence, the blackened metal spikes ringing out as they chewed into the wooden wheels of the cart. Taking advantage of the distraction, Van Helsing threw himself at Sandor in an effort to knock him off balance, only to feel as if he had been dashed against a brick wall. Undaunted, Sandor grasped the front of the student's shirt with one hand and lifted him off his feet. With his free hand, the vampire wound the whip about Van Helsing's throat and tightened it. Van Helsing dug at the lash with his fingers, but the leather was already cutting deep into the skin. The pressure on his windpipe made him feel sure that any moment he was going to retch, only to drown in the refuse.

"Get the reins," Van Helsing gasped, wondering if his raspy voice could be heard above the commotion. "If those rims or spokes splinter we'll...."

The wreck Van Helsing was about to predict happened so quickly that it was over before any of them realized it had even taken place. The whole world whirled, spinning upside down as the cart flipped, throwing Van Helsing and Wellington onto a snowy knoll on the opposite side of the fence. Sandor's body had been a blur as he sprang forward, his hands becoming claws clutching at the driver's seat to keep from being tossed about like a rag doll. His talons dug deep into the seat, only to find himself pinned beneath the cart as it overturned. As the vehicle came crashing down upon the fence, the vampire was impaled upon rows of iron spikes while splintered wood from the wagon tore through his torso.

As Sandor's heart ruptured, Countess Bathory fell back into the deep seat of her carriage, gasping for air and clutching at her chest as if she had received the wound. Her heart beat against her breast as she came out of the trance, and it was several minutes before she could get her eyes to focus. Elga was next to her, one hand over Bathory's, feeling the throb of each pulse as she tried to calm her.

"What is it, Elizabeth? What happened?"

Bathory shook her head. "He's dead, dearest one."

Before Elga could ask her any more, a sharp cry of pain cut her off and brought Elizabeth out of her stupor, all senses alert. Carmilla had collapsed onto the carriage floor, convulsing violently. Elga slid beside her, cradling Carmilla's head in her lap.

"We have to get back," whispered Carmilla. She managed a smile for Elga, seeing her concern. "You were right...I shouldn't have come. I'm still too weak."

“Carmilla needs more blood,” Bathory said. “She should gorge herself and return to her coffin for a few days.” With a sharp rap on the ceiling to signal the driver, the countess brought the coach to a halt. Opening the door, she stepped out, pausing long enough to tell Elga, “Look after your cousin.”

“Where are you going?” Elga asked.

“Hunting. Spielsdorf is nearby; I can smell him.”

“Do you think the two boys are working with him?”

“If they are, their youth and inexperience may give us a chance to destroy the general’s organization from within.” Bathory’s figure began to fade, a phantom form that melted into the night. Her last words were a whisper in the mist. “If they are not, I may find other uses for them.”

When Van Helsing regained consciousness face down on the ground, he was fairly sure that he was not home in bed. Even more distressing to him was that this meant his last waking memories had not been some dark, disturbed dream. He hoped the nearby groan meant Wellington had survived. Wincing at the pain each movement brought, Van Helsing rolled onto his back and slowly, stiffly sat up. Not ten feet away, propped up on one arm as he gingerly rubbed his aching head, was his classmate.

"Any broken bones, Bram?" Wellington asked.

"No.” Van Helsing shook his head. “You?"

"I'm in too much pain to tell."

"Good thing you were wearing your lucky boots."

"Are you going to start that again?"

"*You* lost *my* money in that card game," Van Helsing pointed out, pelting Wellington with a clod of frozen sod. "We weren’t exactly wallowing in wealth at the end of that night, were we? If you'd have been paying more attention to what was in your hand instead of what was on your feet, you might have at least broken even."

"And we’d still be stuck here in the middle of the night in the middle of nowhere." Wellington fell back on the ground and took a deep breath. "Where are we, anyway?"

Brushing himself off as best he could, Van Helsing nodded towards an overturned stone cross. "It seems to be a cemetery."

As realization set in, both men were on their feet, physical discomfort forgotten.

"If anyone heard the crash and went for help, soldiers will be on their way here," Wellington said. "If we're caught in a cemetery after curfew, we'll be staying on as patrons."

Van Helsing dashed towards the damaged fence with Wellington hot at his heels, only to stop dead in his tracks as the initial panic passed. Wellington collided into him, and once more they found themselves sprawled upon the ground.

"What can they hang us for?" Van Helsing asked with a laugh. "We haven't robbed a grave."

"No, but we did steal a body from the morgue."

"But he wasn't dead; that's only kidnapping."

Wellington pondered this. It seemed to make sense. "Speaking of which, where is our passenger?"

"I didn't notice him lying about anywhere. Either he's already gotten away...." Van Helsing's voice trailed off.

"...or he never cleared the cart," Wellington finished the thought.

They covered the remaining ground to the damaged fence and the site of the wreckage, but this time stealthily on their hands and knees, hoping not to attract the attention of anyone who might happen to be out and about on the road. The tangled mass of wood heaped over the twisted section of iron fence was still vaguely recognizable as a cart, but could serve no other purpose than as a future source of firewood. The horse must have escaped unscathed, for there was no sign of it in the brick street.

As they reached the remains of the stolen vehicle, Wellington asked, "Can you see anything?"

"No. If Sandor were here, he'd have heard us and called for help."

"Maybe he's trapped underneath," Wellington suggested.

"Maybe he's alright."

"Maybe you should have a look."

"I knew you were going to say that." Van Helsing used one edge of the cart to steady himself and, ducking under the ragged timber, stuck his head up into the overturned wagon. Not being able to see anything in the dark hulk, he started to reach up to see if he could feel anything when a cold hand struck him in the face. With a cry that nearly deafened him in the enclosed space, Van Helsing quickly rejoined his classmate.

"What is it?" Wellington asked.

"He's in there, stuck like a roasting pig on a spit."

"Now the charge is murder. Shall we just stay and dig the graves ourselves?"

"We didn't kill him," Van Helsing observed. "It was an accident. Our taking him from the morgue may have even helped save his life. He must have been cataleptic; the shock of the cold night air and sleet revived him. If he hadn't attacked us, you would have still been at the reins and we would still be on the road."

"Cataleptic?" Wellington was not convinced.

"What else would explain it?"

“Try explaining those wounds. You saw how they healed. This wasn’t just a case of catalepsy.”

"Any suggestions?" Van Helsing asked.

“We put as much distance as we can between ourselves and here.”

Van Helsing looked at Wellington in disbelief. “That’s it? That’s your grand plan?”

"Of course not; we get our friend here back to the university, and then we get very drunk."

As appealing as the idea was, Van Helsing remained skeptical. "You do realize what time it is? The tavern won’t be open, and even Gretchen wouldn’t let us in at this hour."

“You underestimate me.”

“You underestimate Gretchen.”

“Let’s get him out of there before rigor mortis sets in.”

“If he’s not already frozen solid,” Van Helsing mumbled, unsure of how long they had been unconscious. “Any ideas on how to transport our ‘guest’ to his final destination?”

“We carry him between us. If we run into the night watch, we just tell them he’s had too much too drink and we’re taking him home.”

Van Helsing shook his head. “He’s a little too dead to pass for dead drunk. Let’s try telling the truth.”

“Sounds like *you’ve* had too much to drink.”

“Hear me out. We tell them we found the body at the scene of a coach accident. True. We tell them we’re taking him to one of the doctors at the university. True.”

“And when they notice he’s dead?”

“We just tell them we weren’t sure of his condition,” Van Helsing said with a shrug. “Also true. If they have any more questions, we bring them back here and let them see the wreck for themselves. Good thing you brought the medical kit; we’re going to need that surgical saw.”

Already suspecting the answer and fearing the worst, Wellington still felt compelled to ask “For what?”

“Our silent partner may come quietly, but he won’t come easily. He’s wedged in pretty tight.”

After the better part of an hour, Sandor's body landed with a plop in the moist snow. Van Helsing and Wellington had, with a considerable amount of prying, sawing and swearing, liberated the corpse from the wreckage of the wagon and cemetery fence. Van Helsing kicked the cadaver.

"What are you doing?" Wellington asked.

"Just making sure."

"It's dead, Bram."

Van Helsing sounded doubtful. "That's what we thought the last time."

"Perhaps it was a muscle spasm."

"Rather a long spasm, don't you think?" Van Helsing cautiously prodded the body with the toe of one boot. "Wasn't there a spare blanket in the cart?"

Wellington placed one hand on Van Helsing's shoulder. "While I appreciate your concern for his creature comforts, I believe his current condition relieves you of that burden."

"If we drape the blanket around him, it will make his current condition less obvious to anyone that might see us. Go get it; we've got a long walk ahead of us."

Shaking his head, Wellington started to climb back into the wreckage. "At least the sleet has stopped," he said, trying to sound optimistic.

Beneath the stone archway of the cemetery entrance, General Spielsdorf and Major Arcana sat on horseback and kept vigil in the shadows, taking care not to be seen by the two students. They had followed Van Helsing and Wellington from the morgue, keeping a safe distance behind, nearly losing sight of the cart when the horse bolted during the fight with Sandor.

"Shall we confront them and confiscate the body?" Arcana asked.

"Not just yet." Spielsdorf strained to pick up any piece of conversation from Van Helsing or Wellington that the night breeze plucking at his grey cloak might carry to him. "Sandor's no longer an immediate concern. I'm more worried that this blossoming blasphemy is going to grow deeper roots."

"Those two would-be body snatchers?" Arcana nodded in the direction the young men had disappeared. "Surely neither of them are—"

"No," Spielsdorf cut him off. "Sandor didn't get the chance to infect them. But the ladies seem to have taken a keen interest in the lads."

"What makes you think Bathory's brood even knows who those boys are?"

Spielsdorf looked at his companion, his mouth curving into a humorless smile. "I'd wager my pension we weren't the only ones watching the morgue tonight, nor the only ones to follow that cart here."

"I noticed no one else."

"I would have been surprised if you did." General Spielsdorf gently nudged his horse. "Let's see where our two young friends are off to."

*

Arminius Vambery was an upper level student who had won the coveted position of anatomy assistant, providing him with lodging, meals, and a modest allowance in exchange for cleaning and maintaining the various instruments and facilities required by the dissection rooms. It was while enjoying the comforts of his bed and a deep sleep that a pounding sounded throughout his chambers in back of the university's surgical theatre. Although the student considered himself levelheaded and steady of hand, nothing could have prepared him for the spectacle that waited on his step.

Standing outside in the cold dark November morning, with Sandor propped up between them, a very weary Van Helsing struggled to hold the body steady as Wellington impatiently stamped his feet to keep warm and shouted, "Dammit, Vambery, answer the bloody door!" Again he used Sandor's head to bang on the brass address plate that identified the entrance.

It was a bleary and bewildered anatomy assistant who peered out into the alley. "Good God!" Vambery staggered away from the door as the three figures brushed past him.

"Be a good fellow and see to the horses, will you?" Van Helsing asked over Sandor's shoulder.

Armed against the weather in his robe and slippers, Vambery stepped out into the alley. Shivering, he looked about and then realized there were no horses. After pondering the problem for a moment, he returned inside and tried to decide if it was worth the energy to be angry with them. He would have been hard-pressed, if asked at the time, to say which was more chilling: The weather, or the sight of the corpse on the examining table with jagged chunks of wood sticking out like spikes from its chest.

"What's wrong with him?" Vambery finally managed, never taking his eyes from the new arrival.

Wellington tried to sound casual. “Nothing; just dead.”

"I can see that." Vambery pointed an accusing finger at the body. "You didn't kill him, did you?"

Van Helsing and Wellington exchanged uneasy glances. "Well, there’s some debate about that," Van Helsing offered hesitantly, "but, for the most part, no."

Vambery seemed to be on the verge of collapse and his two schoolmates helped him into a chair. His attention was still fixed upon the impaled specimen. Van Helsing gestured from Sandor to the glassy-eyed anatomy assistant. Wellington nodded and, taking a sheet from a pile of linen in the corner, covered the corpse. The broken boards beneath the dingy cloth gave it the appearance of a grotesque circus tent.

With the body out of actual sight, Vambery slowly looked from the anatomy table to Van Helsing. "Why is all that wood in him, Bram?"

Van Helsing patted the senior student's shoulder. "It’s from the horse cart he was in. It flipped and crashed, pinning him underneath. The poor fellow had an accident, that's all."

Vambery seemed to take comfort in this. “How did you find him?”

“In pretty much the same condition you see him in now,” Wellington replied.

Van Helsing groaned. "Even for you, that was bad."

"You'd have said it if you had thought it."

"I'd never stoop so low."

"You'll never climb so high."

Van Helsing turned to Vambery. "Arminius, you be the judge. Who's the wit?"

"You're both keen," came the deliberate and diplomatic reply, "but each in his own way. Bram, here, is like champagne, while Gerald is like beer. Different tastes, but both intoxicating."

"Well said," laughed Van Helsing.

"Beer travels better," Wellington pointed out. "And in the interests of prolonging lives, especially our own, we might consider calling on Gretchen before we call it a night.”

“It’s now morning,” Van Helsing observed.

"Precisely, which means we’ll just be in time for breakfast."

"If she has breakfast ready and waiting, and you don't fling yourself at her feet and ask her to marry you on the spot, then I will," Van Helsing threatened.

"Aren't you in enough trouble with Christine without proposing marriage to everyone who feeds you?"

“I’ve been invited to lunch, tomorrow, so I seem to have been given absolution…again.”

Wellington looked at his watch. “Don’t you mean lunch today? You don’t want to leave her waiting around all afternoon for you to show up because you can’t keep regular hours.”

"Rather than keep either of your ladies in question waiting," Vambery began, "why not return to their arms, allowing me to return to the arms of Morpheus."

Gerald shook his head. "Arminius, you haven't lived until you've experienced the night."

"I am content to experience seeing you to the door and locking it behind you."

Vambery soon found himself gratefully guestless. After taking a final, groggy peek under the sheet at the body on the examining table, the anatomy assistant shuffled down the hall to his bed. "Many more like this, and I'll switch over to history next season."

It took little time for Vambery to float back to the sea of sleep, buoyed by the hope that his encounter with Van Helsing and Wellington would turn out to be some passing nightmare. Drowning deeply in dreams, he could not hear the scratching sounds that now disturbed the delivery room where Sandor's body lay. There was a pause, then a raspy metallic scraping, followed by a sharp click announcing that the lock of the alley door had been successfully picked. The door opened, and a pair of iron-grey eyes peered in. Seeing the room unoccupied, General Spielsdorf swiftly and silently slipped inside, motioning for Major Arcana to follow.

Spotting the sheet-shrouded form on the examination table, Spielsdorf took the lantern Arcana carried and uncovered the corpse. He leaned close, fingers probing the throat. Although the wounds on Sandor had healed when he revived, there were still faint scars on the flesh from the vampires' bites. "Nosferatu," the General confirmed. "More than one, from the looks of it. He was bled to death in minutes. Bathory and her nieces, no doubt. If only we could have finished them off." Spielsdorf turned away from the body, disgusted more with himself than with the creature beside him. "I was a fool to try to take them that night. The 23rd of this month was the Sabbat of the Undead, when their powers were at their peak."

"The strategy was sound." Arcana plucked with annoyance at the gold cord on the hilt of his saber. "Catch them by surprise, when their confidence was high...."

"Yes, and rightfully so, it would seem. Carmilla survived and Elga escaped us. As for Bathory, she is too much the fox to be taken so easily. I should have destroyed Elga when I had the chance. I thought by using her as bait, we could draw the other two out of hiding. I hadn't counted on them using the elements against us, forcing us indoors." The general turned back to Sandor. "Or on some wayward traveler releasing her. The cost of a miscalculation in this battle is high, and I've paid the price...again."

"He is dead now, isn't he?"

"Yes, but not by any cleverness on our part. Come on, it will be sunrise soon." Spielsdorf began to lift the body up from the table. "The ancient vampires dissolve upon true death, crumbling to dust as they should have long ago. One this new will undergo the process naturally, over the same period of time as any recently deceased. I cannot run the risk of someone or something removing those bits of wood before it has completely decomposed. We must cremate the body and scatter the ashes."

Working quickly and quietly, the two men carried Sandor out of the room. Out in the alley, Arcana slung the body across Spielsdorf's horse as the older man held the animal, speaking softly to it as he rubbed its nose to keep the beast from bolting away with its unholy burden. Securing the corpse in place, Arcana asked, "How long will you wage this war?" He regretted the question even as the words came from his tongue, and blamed his lack of diplomacy on lack of sleep. The first two vampires he and Spielsdorf had destroyed had been victims of Countess Bathory. They had been the General's wife and daughter.

After several seconds of silence, Spielsdorf finally spoke. "As long as I live."

*

“Chin up, Bram,” Wellington said as they stumbled through the street. “We’re almost there.”

“I’m too tired to eat,” Van Helsing protested. “Why couldn’t you just let me go to bed?”

“And eat alone? You don’t want Gretchen to think you’re snubbing her, do you?”

“I’m exhausted, not an idiot. With me there, Gretchen’s less likely to take you to task for taking her for granted.”

“Excuse me,” a voice called from behind them.

Turning, Van Helsing and Wellington were surprised to find a woman on horseback in the street behind them. Neither had heard hooves approaching on the snow-covered cobblestones. Although most of her features were hidden by the hood of her cloak and the long blonde curls that flowed down to cover the lower half of her face, even in the dim grey light of morning they could make out a pair of wolfish blue eyes peering down at them.

“The two of you look like healthy young lads, and I’m afraid this night has left me ravenous.” The laughter in Bathory’s eyes went unnoticed by the students. “Perhaps you could recommend one of the local establishments to a weary traveler?”

“The food at the Wolf’s Head is popular with the students and staff of the university,” Wellington said, turning to point in the direction of the tavern that had been their own destination.

"We do seem to spend a lot of time and money there." Van Helsing cast a critical eye on his friend, adding, "Of course, the fact that his girlfriend happens to work there has little bearing on the matter."

As the two turned to invite the stranger to join them, they found the street empty. Looking about, Van Helsing frowned at what he saw on the ground. The only footprints in the snow were their own.

4. Deception and Disappointment.

It was difficult to tell if the frost on the university windows came from the winter air, or from the reception that awaited Abraham Van Helsing and Gerald Wellington inside the chambers of the Anatomy Council. A formal summons had been sent to the students' rooms just before noon, demanding an immediate audience. Seated at a long refectory table, Dr. Belasko, Dr. Hunyadi and Dr. Matthias stared balefully at the students as they were shown into the room. In spite of Belasko's slight look of disappointment, the general impression was that of three vultures waiting to feast upon their flesh.

After what seemed an infinity of silence, Van Helsing ventured, "You wanted to see us?"

"Do we want to see you?" With considerable control over the rage boiling within him, Matthias managed a smug smile. "To be blunt, never seeing *either* of you again is a concept I find most appealing, if not altogether seductive."

"I'm afraid we don't understand...." Wellington looked from Matthias to Belasko, who sat tight-lipped and tense.

"It would appear to be a shared ignorance." Belasko met the young man's gaze and then looked away, dejected. "I thought, after our little talk yesterday morning, I had awakened some sense of responsibility in you. I obviously overestimated one of us."

Van Helsing resented being spoken to as a child. "I admit that, as a student, I am not the most disciplined fellow to ever enter these halls, nor am I the most dense. With due respect, what are you trying to say?"

"Au revoir. Auf Wiedersehen. Adieu." For the first time since they had met him, Dr. Matthias actually seemed gleeful. "As of this moment, your career here has been terminated for the duration of the academic calendar. You may, if you so desire, apply next fall...."

"That's nearly a year away," Van Helsing protested. "What have we done to deserve dismissal?"

"What *haven't* you done would be more easily answered," Hunyadi replied. "Were you or were you not charged with delivering a specimen for dissection purposes as a token of atonement?"

"Yes, we were...and we *did*." The doctors' silence declared their doubt, prompting Wellington to continue. "Ask Vambery, he took the delivery."

"We have already conferred with Master Vambery. He tells us you brought in a body so peppered with splinters that it looked like a porcupine." Matthias raised his hands to silence the students. "How the unfortunate fellow came to have more wood in him than Pinocchio is, I am sure, a tale worth the telling. It is even possible, however improbable, that you actually found the corpse in question already in such a wretched state. Unfortunately, I fear we must be spared the spellbinding narrative. Stealing a body for the university is one thing, but stealing it *from* the university is another matter altogether. I don't know what sort of game you're up to, but it's over. And so are your studies for this session."

Van Helsing and Wellington looked at each other in disbelief.

"What would we do with a corpse?" Wellington demanded.

Matthias looked as if he had been asked to describe God. "Given the inclinations of your imaginations, I shudder to think...especially after finding that book by the Shelley woman in your possession."

"We didn't take the body from the university," Van Helsing insisted.

Belasko looked over the rim of his glasses at the two young men. "Am I to take it he just got up and walked away?"

"That's what happened at the morgue," Wellington blurted out without thinking. "He was going to kill Bram, but I grabbed the whip and...."

Unable to contain his temper, Matthias, who had been taking notes throughout the interview, tossed his pen aside. "What do you take us for, fools?" Both students resisted the urge to answer. "Killer cadavers, walking dead, and whips? What were you saying about whips?"

As Wellington started to answer he saw Van Helsing shake his head slightly in silent warning. "Nothing, sir," Wellington said, defeated. "You wouldn't believe it."

Matthias' eyebrows raised in astonishment. "Perhaps you fear it might reduce the credibility of your earlier narrative? Come, gentlemen; indulge us."

Wellington looked at Van Helsing, who shrugged. There was nothing left to lose. "I had this whip...."

"Yes, a common instrument amongst anatomists," Dr. Hunyadi said dryly.

"I didn't bring the whip with me. Earlier in the evening, we had to steal a cart and horse...."

"The least of your offenses, I'm sure." Matthias observed.

"I did say you wouldn't believe it."

"But feel certain we'll have no trouble digesting the rest of this nonsense!" Matthias was on his feet. "If I find you within the walls of the city during the remainder of the term, your suspension from this institution will be permanent."

The sun glared harshly on the snow as Van Helsing and Wellington trudged out into the street in front of the university. Van Helsing tried to sound positive. "At least they gave us until the end of the week to vacate our rooms."

"Thanks to Professor Belasko. You did say we've yet to be exiled from England, didn't you?"

"Do you really want to live that close to your parents again?" Van Helsing asked.

"There's little choice, unless we waste the rest of this school year. I rather fancy graduating before becoming a grandfather."

Van Helsing looked out into the street but, lost in thought, his eyes were unseeing. He suddenly snapped out of his reverie. "Why start over again somewhere else if we can pick up where we left off here? If we can prove our story, the university would have to reinstate us."

"While I admire your optimistic outlook, does the expression 'Clutching at straws' mean anything to you?"

"Hear me out," Van Helsing insisted. "Remember what Dr. Bell taught us about objective observation leading to deduction and diagnosis? Sandor said something about blood...your blood. From its smell he could tell you were English, and quoted the old line from Mother Goose...or was it the Brothers Grimm?"

"Grim would be more in keeping with our situation." Wellington was skeptical. "Maybe he just heard my voice, and used the accent to place my nationality."

"Okay, *maybe*. But we both saw physical evidence that Sandor had been attacked. He had been bitten savagely and repeatedly, from more than one person."

"Animal," Wellington corrected.

"Person," pressed Van Helsing. "Remember the jaw span and arrangement of teeth. Either way, man or animal, he was killed by something that took most of his blood."

"He wasn't dead."

"What?"

"He wasn't dead," Wellington repeated. "He was in shock, if not from the attack, then from exposure and severe blood loss. As much as he was tossed about in the back of that cart, the stimulation revived him."

"So why did he attack us?"

"He had no idea how long he'd been unconscious. That fits in with your theory that another person bit him. Look at it from the victim's point-of-view: A couple of strangers ambush Sandor, start feeding on him, and he faints. When he comes to, he's in the back of a cart driven by the two of us. Naturally, he's going to think we're the ones who were nibbling on him."

"Not bad," conceded Van Helsing, "but you've overlooked a minor point. We both saw the bite marks heal in a matter of seconds. Explain that. And keep in mind Sandor had a forest of splinters in him when we left his body at the university. No doubt about death then, so what happened to him?"

"Vambery?"

"No, I don't think he'd have the heart to hurt us; he knows the trouble we were already in. And I'm sure that band of merry men we just left have put him through the inquisition. If there were any suspicions he had been playing a prank, he would have been in there with us. Even if Vambery were the culprit, there would still be the phenomenon of Sandor's wounds healing right before our eyes. Where was he killed?"

"Not far from Klausenburg."

"Then we retrace his steps."

"To Klausenburg? Why?"

"To find out what happened to him that night. If we can hand the council proof that what we've told them is true, we're back in Buda-Pest."

"What if, while following his footsteps, we follow his fate as well?"

"Sandor was probably ambushed, but we know to expect trouble on the road. Besides, how many people do you know as handy with a blade or a brace of pistols as we are?" Van Helsing nudged Wellington's shoulder, and saw from the look on his friend's face that his spirits were contagious.

"When do you want to start? I'll need to tell Gretchen goodbye."

"That will probably be the most dangerous part of the whole trip. I've promised to take Christine to the theatre tomorrow night; I don't dare break that date."

"Then we'll set out for Klausenburg the morning after. I'll leave word with Vambery to look after our things."

"We'll need to arrange for horses."

"Leave that to me," Wellington said.

"Leave that to Gretchen, you mean."

A passing coach splattered them with slush.

"This day just keeps getting better," Van Helsing sighed, wiping trying to brush his cloak clean. "I'm afraid to guess what happens next."

"That's easily answered." Wellington produced a decanter of cognac from the folds of his cloak. "We get drunk."

"Tell me you didn't steal that from Matthias' office."

"He can only expel us once, and he's already done that."

General Spielsdorf and Major Arcana were halfway through their midday meal when Lieutenant Markus arrived at the hotel's dining room. The younger officer stood to one side of the door, waiting until Spielsdorf took notice and motioned him over to the table. As Markus approached, Spielsdorf's gaze fell upon a middle-aged man who watched him from the lobby.

"I found the medical officer you wanted," Markus said.

Spielsdorf's gaze never left the man watching him. "So I see."

Markus turned to the man in question and gave a curt nod, upon which he left the lobby to join them. Upon this newcomer's arrival at the table, Spielsdorf gave a quick sweep of his hand in silent invitation for he and Markus to be seated. The general kept the introductions brief. "Major Arcana, this is Dr. Arnaud Paole, my regiment's former surgeon before he decided to return to civilian life here in Buda-Pest."

"I received your letter," Paole said. "And your suspicions are correct; the Bathory family had an ancestral home in this region."

Arcana gave a short, involuntary laugh. "So that's how you knew this is where she would be."

"She has few familiar places left to flee," Spielsdorf said, nodding. "After we discovered her sanctuary at the Scholomance and burnt the place to the ground, she needed a new stronghold. Her castle at Csejte was left in ruins over a century ago, and we got too close to her in Klausenburg for her to risk remaining there. Nor was she likely to choose her childhood homes at Nyirbator or Ecsed, as they would be too obvious. No; she would seek out a refuge that was old and obscure, someplace that predated even her own birth."

"I fear I may disappoint you," Paole cautioned. "Archives from that far back are rarely ever complete. And after the scandal and trial, most references to the countess were purged from public records. Whatever may remain of the family castle, its location does not appear on any map that I've been able to find."

There was quiet confidence in Spielsdorf's voice. "I've yet to come across a fox that can't be tracked back to its lair."

"A cornered fox is a dangerous fox," Markus observed. "It would be better to take Bathory on neutral ground."

Spielsdorf's ice-cold eyes locked onto those of his lieutenant. "There is no neutral ground in the war between Good and Evil."

Elga moved silently through the wind-swept streets, oblivious to the increasing cold and gathering gloom that evening brought with it. In spite of her insensitivity to the physical world, she was acutely aware that her cousin Carmilla was close at hand. Aunt Elizabeth described the ability as a territorial instinct that allowed vampires to sense when others of their kind were about, even permitting them to identify an individual of their own bloodline. And there was a certain feral quality to Carmilla that made her readily recognizable without the benefit of an enhanced sensory system.

Hardly had that last thought entered Elga's mind when she saw the blood-splattered snow at the mouth of an alley just ahead. The splintered remains of a wooden tray surrounded by scattered nuts and sweets told her that a street vendor had been Carmilla's latest feast. Looking about to be sure she was alone, Elga dashed toward the alley. Barely had she reached the entrance when a girl in her late teens staggered out, her eyes wild and pleading.

"Help me," the girl gasped, collapsing into Elga's arms.

The scent of blood was in the air, and Elga resisted the impulse to feed in such a public place. Her eyes went to the pulsing vein in the girl's neck, the flesh so pale in contrast to her dark hair, and her mouth went dry as the muscles in the base of her throat tightened with temptation. Elga leaned closer, her lips not quite touching her victim's skin but still close enough to feel the flesh just beneath them.

"Help me," came a voice from the shadows of the alley. It was the same voice Elga had heard from the girl she now embraced. Looking toward the source of the sound, she saw a girl slowly crawling across the snow-covered cobblestones toward her; a girl identical to the one in her arms. Elga's attention was so focused on this newcomer that she did not notice the change taking place in her intended victim. At the sound of laughter from the girl she held, Elga looked down to find the young woman's hair growing lighter and longer while her gaunt cheeks filled out and grew flush with fresh blood.

"Carmilla!" Elga shoved her cousin away from her.

Still laughing, Carmilla sat up in the snow. "Now is that lady-like?"

Elga looked from Carmilla to her dying victim, and then back at her cousin again. In spite of her annoyance, there was a hint of curiosity in her voice. "Where did you learn *that* trick?"

"In one of those musty old books Aunt Elizabeth brought with us."

"You know we're not allowed in the library."

Carmilla pretended to pout. "I thought you would be pleased that I was trying to improve my education." Suddenly she leaned forward to speak in an urgent whisper, "Did you know we could assume the appearance of anyone we've fed upon?"

Elga looked over at the remains of Carmilla's meal, who now lay face down in the snow regarding the two of them with lifeless eyes. Finally she returned her attention to Carmilla. "Do it again."

"I can't," Carmilla said, shaking her head. "It only works while the victim is still alive. Even then it's limited. Once their blood has been completely digested, we lose the ability." Carmilla's mouth curved into a wicked smile. "Imagine meeting someone who caught your fancy; you could appear to them in the guise of their lover."

"You would think of that."

"What's the point of being what we are if you won't take advantage of it? You might as well still be alive—" Barely had the last word left her lips when Carmilla winced in pain and clutched at her left shoulder where the Kukri knife had almost cut her to the bone three nights earlier. Glistening like a liquid ruby, a single tear of blood trickled down her cheek.

"You've tried to do too much too soon," Elga chastised.

Carmilla tried to sound cavalier. "Lucky for me you happened to come along."

"Luck has nothing to do with it; Aunt Elizabeth sent me to find you and bring you back. You're to spend the rest of the night in your coffin."

"The whole night?" Carmilla grew petulant.

"She's afraid you'll go roaming about and attract the attention of General Spielsdorf and his men…*again*."

"Klausenburg wasn't my fault."

"Nothing is ever your fault." Elga stood up and brushed the snow from her clothes. "Coming?"

"Do I have a choice?"

"Yes, you can stay here until Aunt Elizabeth comes for you…." Elga stretched out her arms as if to embrace the elements and the wind whipped up around her, billowing her cloak out like enormous wings. Flesh and cloth dissolved into the night, leaving Carmilla alone. Elga's last words were a whisper echoed throughout the empty street, "…if you really want your coffin to be used for its original purpose."

The snow had started as a few dry wisps at dusk, only to grow heavier with thick wet clinging flakes, quickly encrusting the city with white crystal and making travel by foot slow and slippery. By the time Van Helsing and Wellington arrived at the Wolf's Head the shutters had already been secured over the glazed windows of the tavern, the wild winter weather having sent customers scurrying home early. Although the public house had been closed for several hours and the innkeeper probably home in bed, Gretchen would still be inside cleaning up after the evening's clientele.

Wellington peered through a chink in one of the shutters and saw the girl behind the bar as she washed tankards, her face half-hidden by the honey-colored hair that tumbled across it. It was the flirtatious way Gretchen's wild green eyes peered out from beneath that silken mane that had attracted his attention that first week in Buda-Pest.

"Has she gone for the night?" Van Helsing asked, checking his pocket watch as he stamped his feet to keep warm.

"She's still there, looking busy and beautiful." Wellington rapped sharply on the tavern door. "Gretchen, it's Gerald. Let me in before I freeze to death."

"Coming, Woolums," came Gretchen's cheery voice.

"'Woolums?'" Van Helsing repeated. "She calls you 'Woolums?'"

"She says I keep her warm." Taking advantage of Van Helsing's momentary loss for words, Wellington tried to guide the conversation toward a more practical course. "Listen, not a word to her about what happened today."

"Whatever you say, Woolums."

"Don't start with me."

The door opened and Gretchen greeted him with, "Let's see about getting you thawed out—oh, hello, Bram!"

"Gretchen." Van Helsing nodded, smiling more in muffled mirth than in greeting. He had to give the girl credit; if she was embarrassed at her exchange with Wellington being overheard, she covered it far more successfully than his roommate did. The rose of her cheeks paled before the blood blazing in Wellington's face.

With her hands on her hips, Gretchen stood in the doorway, silently challenging them to pass, but the glint in her eye and the curl of her mouth meant mischief rather than a reprimand. "What are you lads doing out so late on a night like this?" Her face softened into a pout. "And just where have you been all evening that you couldn't come and see me earlier?"

Before Wellington could speak, Van Helsing started to answer for him. "Well, it's funny you should ask. You see, Woolums and I were...." He stopped short as Gretchen arched one eyebrow skeptically.

"Is this something I really want to hear?" she asked.

"No," the two friends intoned.

"Is this something I'd even believe?"

"No," came the chorus.

"I'm not even sure I believe it," Wellington added.

Gretchen shook her head tolerantly and stepped back inside. "Get in here, the two of you."

As Van Helsing and Wellington crossed the threshold and the flickering light of the tavern spilled across them, the barmaid's mouth and eyes widened in disbelief. She caught both of them by the collar. "Look at you! Just look at yourselves. Do either of you own a mirror?"

Both students looked at each other. Looking back at Gretchen, Wellington smiled. "I'd much rather look at you."

Gretchen ignored the compliment. "Your clothes and hair are a mess. If it weren't for the wind, I'd say you've been out brawling again." Before either of them could respond, the barmaid whirled on Van Helsing. "I expect it from *him*, but you usually show a little more common sense. Do you know Christine has been in three times tonight looking for you?"

"I don't believe it," sighed Van Helsing, leaning against the door to let the weight of his body close it. He felt exhausted as the day's events began to take their toll.

Gretchen's eyes narrowed into wintry slits. "I may have lied *for* you, but I've never lied *to* you."

"No," Van Helsing shook his head, "I meant I don't believe this night could actually have gotten worse. I was supposed to call on her this evening but, after our audience with Dr. Belasko this morning, I forgot all about it."

"Belasko," echoed Gretchen. "You two are in trouble again, aren't you? What now?"

"It's nothing." Wellington moved towards a table but was brought to a halt by Gretchen's voice.

"Let me see your boots," she insisted.

"What?"

"I don't want you mucking the place up after I've spent the last two hours sweeping." As the two students painfully pulled off their boots and left them by the door, Gretchen took down chairs from the top of a table near the bar. Going behind the counter, she produced two glasses and asked, "Schnapps?"

"Good enough." Wellington sank gratefully into one of the chairs.

"It's better than you deserve." Gretchen placed the glasses and a bottle before them and then stood there, wistful and quiet, her arms folded across her chest.

"Aren't you going to join us?" Wellington asked.

"I might, if you're nice to me…and can account for having avoided me all evening."

Wellington's hand paused in mid-arc as he started to light a cigar. "But you'll drink with us if we promise to do proper penance?"

"If I wait for *you* to do proper penance, I'll die of thirst." Gretchen gave him a knowing nudge with her hip before dancing her way into the storeroom behind the bar. A moment later she called out, "We just had a shipment of black cherry wine from Germany this afternoon, but I'm not going to waste it on the likes of you. It's too sweet to guzzle."

Van Helsing and Wellington exchanged an approving glance as the latter asked, "How old is it?"

"As if you could tell vintage from vinegar," came Gretchen's reply from the storeroom.

"At least I have a discriminating palate where you're concerned."

"Aren't I the lucky one, then?"

Before Gretchen returned, Wellington motioned Van Helsing to lean closer to avoid being overheard. In an urgent whisper he said, "Not a word to her about our trip to Klausenburg."

"How are you going to explain our sudden need for horses?"

"I'll think of something."

Van Helsing took out his watch and again checked the time. "You've got a day to weave your latest yarn." He sat the timepiece on the table to keep track of the hour. His gaze came to rest on the miniature portrait of his fiancée mounted in the inner cover of the watchcase. "After what happened at the university today, Christine will be ready to have me buried in quicklime...alive!"

"Be glad she's studying to be a schoolmistress and not an anatomist. The concept of vivisection has yet to be brought to her attention."

Gretchen reappeared, a bottle of wine in her hand. Taking a goblet as she passed by the bar, she sat in a chair between Wellington and Van Helsing. "Now, what was all this whispering while I was away?" Before either of them could reply, there came a knock at the front door. "I'm doing more business after hours than when we were open." Going to the windows, the barmaid peeked out. Smiling to herself, Gretchen threw back the bolt and opened the door. "Back again, Chris?"

Van Helsing felt his heart skip a beat at the sound of her voice as Christine asked, "Has Bram stopped by?"

"He just got here, along with that worthless friend of his." Gretchen stepped back from the door. "Come in and get warm."

As Van Helsing looked up into those dark eyes smoldering beneath her bangs, something told him Christine had probably not noticed the cold. "Chris...." was all he had time to say.

"I should have known." Her words chilled him more than any winter wind. "You have time enough to sit here drinking, but not time enough to come and see me."

"I'm sorry." Van Helsing's throat was suddenly very dry.

"Very sorry, I should think." Christine took the chair Gretchen offered. The barmaid filled the glass she had brought out for herself and gave it to the girl to calm her. Christine noticed the watch lying open on the table. At the sight of the tiny oval portrait of her mounted inside, she said, "At least you found room for me somewhere in your life. You promised to have dinner with Frau

Snell and I at the school. I sat there the whole evening, waiting. Can you imagine what the rest of the girls will be saying tomorrow? When you still hadn't called after supper, I was afraid something had happened to you. I've been out all night trying to find you. You weren't here; you weren't at your rooms. If the director or the headmistress finds I've left the grounds at this hour, you know what could happen to me?"

"It can't be any worse than what's happened to us." Wellington reached for the bottle of schnapps, but stopped short at Van Helsing's icy stare.

Christine turned on him, her raven hair flowing like liquid night. "Not all of us want to spend the rest of our lives as students." Returning her attention to Van Helsing, she asked, "What kind of trouble are you in this time?"

"It's nothing," Van Helsing assured her. "We've been through this sort of thing before."

"So it's as bad as all that?"

"It's nothing, really." Van Helsing took her hands. "Promise me you won't worry. I don't want you getting upset."

"Careful, Bram," Wellington said as Gretchen sat on the arm of his chair. "This could work to your advantage. I've always found a frightened female to be quite negotiable."

"You're an absolute ass at times," the barmaid pointed out. "Do you know that?"

"I think they're something of a matched set, Gretchen." Christine emptied her glass, and the other girl refilled it.

Gretchen cast a critical eye over Wellington. "Yet we're the ones foolish enough to stay with them, although I can't imagine why."

"I can think of a reason or two," Wellington said, pulling Gretchen onto his lap.

"Minor reasons, perhaps."

Wellington's cheeks burned as his face turned red. Hoping to direct attention away from himself, he nodded at Van Helsing and asked, "But why do you waste your evenings on him, Chris? Van Helsing, the eternal virgin."

"Rather telling about a man that can keep a girl happy with his trousers up, isn't it?" Gretchen took Wellington's cigar and extinguished it in his drink. "What do you think, Christine?"

"I don't know what to think anymore." Christine finished her wine. Standing, she began to button her cloak and glanced at Van Helsing. "I'd like to get at least a little sleep before the night is over. Why don't you walk me back to the school?"

"He can't," Wellington piped up. Left alone with Christine, he knew Van Helsing would eventually tell the girl everything that had happened that morning.

Christine looked accusingly from one student to the other. "Why?"

Van Helsing was silent. Again it was Wellington who spoke. "We've got to deliver some supplies to the university," he lied, hoping to keep either of the girls from guessing they had been expelled.

Pain and suspicion burned fiercely in Christine's eyes. "At this hour? You must think me the most simple-minded girl that ever lived." She turned to Van Helsing, but he could not meet her gaze. "I don't know what it is the two of you are up to, but I do know this: We have tickets for the theatre tomorrow night. If you embarrass me again like you did tonight, you needn't bother calling on me anymore."

Van Helsing started to follow Christine as she turned to leave, but Gretchen was on her feet, shoving him gently but firmly back into his chair. Walking together to the door, the women spoke for several minutes before Christine, with a glance back at Van Helsing, left. Gretchen locked the door and returned to the table, sitting in the chair Christine had been in. Reaching for the wine, the barmaid drank straight from the bottle, letting the taste fill her mouth before slowly swallowing. No one looked at each other.

Gretchen appeared deep in thought for a moment, started to speak, and then hesitated before finally making up her mind. "One day, the two of you are going to have to grow up. Bram, we've known each other for a long time, and I've never interfered in your affairs. I'm telling you this as a friend; Chris is tired, and she's cold, and she's angry, and if you're not careful, you're going to lose her. You can only hurt a girl so many times before she stops coming back." Gretchen cast a critical look at Wellington. "We're not pets who have to rely on you."

There was silence. No one spoke. No one moved. Finally, Wellington slid Van Helsing's watch across the top of the table to see the time. He leaned towards the girl and brushed the hair from her brow. "Gretchen, this is very important. We need a couple of horses for the morning after tomorrow, but you cannot say anything to anyone…not even Christine."

Gretchen looked at him, her countenance darkening. "Do you want to tell me about it?"

"I can't explain things right now."

"No, I rather thought you couldn't."

"If ever I've needed your help, this is that time."

"If things don't change, this may be the last time." Gretchen freed his fingers from her hair and kissed the palm of his hand. "I'll have the horses ready. Now I've got to get back to work. You're welcome to stay and enjoy the warmth for a while longer." She stood, shaking her head tolerantly. "I don't know where the two of you are going, or why, but those horses better come back without a scratch or there are going to be two new bodies for the dissection class."

As Christine walked along the silent snowy streets, she began to hear the faint echo of distant hoofbeats. Had she turned at the sound, she would have seen the ebony coach and team of black horses materializing in the street behind her. Barely had the spectral carriage taken on physical form when the air was suddenly filled with the clatter of its hooves and wheels. Startled, Christine darted out of its path. No sooner had she stepped onto the sidewalk than the coach halted at her side.

The door to the carriage was flung open and a woman whisked out, almost as breathless with excitement as Christine as she asked the girl, “Oh dearest one, are you hurt? Travel by night, especially in this weather, is so dangerous because you absolutely cannot see anything until you are almost on top of it.”

“I’m…I’m fine, thank you,” Christine managed. She smiled at the concern in the woman’s eyes, and found herself not wanting to look away from them. Dimly, in the back of her mind, it occurred to Christine that the woman’s cloak was almost the same shade of blue as her eyes.

“Are you in trouble, my child? A young girl should not be out on the streets alone, certainly not at this hour. Where are you going on a night like this?”

“I’m fine,” Christine said, unaware she was repeating herself. Those eyes were such a light hue that the blue almost seemed ablaze. “I was on my way back to the Snell Academy for Young Women.”

The woman glanced in the direction Christine had come from. Looking back at the girl, she gave her a knowing smile.

"What could have possibly brought you out on such a frosty evening? A young man, perhaps?"

Christine started to speak, only to find that she did not want to tell the stranger about her boyfriend. There was something sinister about her. Was it the eyes? The smile?

"Come," the woman indicated her carriage. "I cannot allow you to walk alone all the way back to the academy." Christine was about to protest when their eyes met again. She was unable to resist as the woman took her gently by the arm and helped her step up into the coach. "You shall get there much quicker by horse than by foot."

As the two of them settled into their seats, the coach lurched forward. The woman's eyes never left Christine, yet the experience left the girl more weary than uncomfortable. "You have yet to tell me your name, child." The remark was a reminder rather than a reprimand.

"Christine."

"Well, Christine, I am the Countess Bathory." There was a pause and a smile. "But you can call me Elizabeth." Those eyes bore deep into her for several seconds before Bathory spoke again, her voice soft and concerned. "Something is troubling you. What is it?"

"How do you know that?"

"I can see it in your eyes; poets say those are the windows to our souls."

Christine smiled, but the expression was bittersweet. "My fiancé and I had a fight."

"Nothing serious, I hope?"

"No…but I think that's the problem; he's not serious enough about the serious things."

Bathory nodded. "Would I know the young man?"

"Probably not; he's a student here at the university. His name is Van Helsing, Abraham Van Helsing."

"I'm not familiar with the name."

"His family comes from Amsterdam." Christine glanced out the carriage window at the darkened shop windows. "We were going to live there after the wedding." Returning her attention to her host, she found herself again staring into those deep blue eyes.

"He sounds like a fascinating fellow," Bathory said, leaning forward in her seat. Darkness swallowed Christine, warm comfortable darkness, as Bathory's voice whispered in her ear, "You must tell me more about him; I want to know *everything*…and then, I want you to forget."

5. Hearts Apart.

Christine turned up the flame in the lamp on her desk at the academy. The soft warm light made the painted roses on lamp's frosted glass glow cheerfully, sending the shadows of the chamber back into the corners of her room. Sitting in the chair, Christine opened the lap door of the desk and pulled out the miniature portrait of Van Helsing she kept there and laid it near her elbow so that she could glance at it as she worked on her daily reports. For several seconds the only sound in the room was the scratching of her pen against paper and the welcome crackle of the fireplace. Then came a gentle knock at her door.

"Come in," Christine called.

The door opened to reveal Tereza Snell, the wife of the headmaster, standing in the corridor. Although she could see no one else, Christine was dimly aware of someone in the shadows behind the older woman.

"Frau Snell," Christine greeted her with a slight nod of her head.

"Christine, we have a visitor," Frau Snell said, stepping inside the room to allow a young woman come in behind her. The girl appeared to be Christine's age, and her dark eyes glistened in the lamplight, which gave a fiery tint to her auburn hair. "This is Countess Karnstein."

"Please," the girl said, visibly uncomfortable with such a formal address, "call me Carmilla."

"I didn't realize any of the Karnsteins were still living," Christine said, only to quickly correct her lack of decorum by adding, "I mean I didn't realize any of them were still living in this area."

Carmilla smiled, but there was something slightly harsh in the expression. "It is an old family, and our numbers are few these days."

Frau Snell patted Carmilla on the shoulder. "Well, they do say quality is more important than quantity. Carmilla's aunt is considering enrolling her niece here with our academy next season, and has written us to ask if she might stay on for the next few days to see if our resources will meet her needs. I was wondering, Christine, if she might room with you during her visit…?"

"Of course!" Christine stood and took Carmilla by the hands. "It will be wonderful to have someone to talk to at night!"

"Excellent!" Frau Snell beamed. "I'll send word to Countess Bathory that you are to be our guest."

Christine frowned and she suddenly felt as if she were far away, only faintly aware of the room around her. "Bathory?" The name was familiar and, while she was sure she should know it, it remained a dim and distant memory.

"Do you know my aunt?" Carmilla asked.

"No, of course not." One of Christine's hands went to her forehead while the other clutched the back of her chair to steady herself. "How could I?"

Carmilla stepped forward, her face full of concern. "Are you unwell?"

"I'm fine…I just…." Christine's voice trailed off.

"You just eat like a bird," Frau Snell insisted, helping Christine back into her chair. She turned to Carmilla and added, "Her young gentleman is coming to call for her this evening, and she hardly touched her dinner. No doubt trying to keep herself pale and thin in hopes he'll find her even more attractive."

Carmilla smiled, her eyes focused intently on Christine. "I think she looks as beautiful as a China doll." Her hand went out to gently caress the girl's cheek, only to quickly pull it away as Christine shuddered under her cool touch. "But much softer and warmer." Catching sight of the miniature portrait on the desk, Carmilla picked it up. "Is this the young gentleman that causes you to risk your health? I must admit I admire your taste; he looks good enough to eat."

Frau Snell shook her head. "In my day, a girl didn't starve herself. A good man appreciates a healthy woman. Your young Van Helsing may be studying to become a doctor, but the last thing he'll want is for his wife to become his first patient. Besides, a woman who looks hungry looks like she can't cook. What if you pass out in the theatre?"

"You're going to the theatre?" Carmilla asked, her excitement showing in her eyes.

"Yes." Christine returned her smile.

"If you can call that sort of thing theatre," Frau Snell said, rolling her eyes. What is it you're going to see, *The Flying Dutchman*?"

"*Faust*," Christine corrected her.

“Either way, it’s hardly a suitable subject for an entertainment. All those ghosts and goings-on....” Frau Snell left the thought unfinished as she turned to leave. “I hope Carmilla’s first night with us won’t be spent saving you from your nightmares.”

“You needn’t worry about that, Frau Snell” Carmilla said, slipping a protective arm about Christine. “With me here, dreams are the last thing she need fear.”

*

The snow whirled in a wintry waltz about the streets as the carriage pulled up before the theatre. The two passengers hardly noticed the crisp cold air, which evaporated before the gaiety that greeted them. The lights and color of the place and its patrons in their evening best spilled out into the night, a pool of warmth in a sea of ice. The carriage had barely stopped when Abraham Van Helsing vaulted out, motioning for his companion to follow. Christine started to step down from the vehicle, then paused and extended her hand to him. Rather than take her offered hand, Van Helsing grabbed her by the waist and spun around, depositing her on the walk. Her feet on the ground, Christine found her hands clasped in his as he danced her up to the entrance of the theatre, oblivious to the stares of the others waiting to attend the performance. The young couple burst into laughter and Christine pressed herself closer to him.

"You seem more like yourself tonight, Bram." She caressed his face with one gloved hand. "I was beginning to think you had forgotten how much fun we used to have together."

"Well, if I ever *do* forget, make sure you remind me."

"Shall I tell you, or show you?" There was a look of hunger behind the humor in her eyes.

Van Helsing sensed where the conversation was leading. "We'll discuss that later." Taking Christine by the elbow, he led her through the main doors and into the foyer of the theatre. "I am still amazed that you would want to see *Faust*."

"I thought it was the only cultural piece I could coax you into taking me. I can never show my face at the opera again...not after you fell asleep and the tenor had to sing over your snoring."

Neither noticed, in the street behind them, the large black coach stopping before the theatre. Dismounting from his perch at the rear of the vehicle, a footman stepped to the side of the carriage as the door swung silently open. "Patience, Elga," came a voice from within.

"Yes, Aunt Elizabeth," sighed the disembodied reply.

The footman reached up to aid his mistress and Countess Bathory stepped out, her eyes and ears taking in every sight and sound. After a moment's pause, she stepped to one side to allow her niece to join her. As the servant closed the door, Bathory asked, "You did secure a private box?"

"Yes, Countess," the footman bowed his head. "Three chairs, just as you instructed, in hopes that Lady Carmilla would have been well enough to accompany you. The tickets are being held at the box office, under your name."

With the countess in the lead, Elga and Elizabeth entered the theatre. Even as she glanced about, smiling and speaking pleasantries to the ladies and gentlemen who greeted her, Bathory's attention was never far from Van Helsing and the young girl on his arm.

"He's very handsome," Elga observed. "His eyes are always laughing."

"Who, dearest one?" Bathory's tone was casually inquiring, to cover her concern.

"The young man ahead of us, the one called Van Helsing. He was at the morgue the other night." Elga turned to look at her aunt and asked, "He's why we've come here tonight, isn't he?"

"What makes you say that?"

"You've taught me not to believe in coincidence. He is here, and so are we. Besides, how many times can you sit through *Faust*? Any lesson it could teach is long lost to us."

Bathory hugged the girl. "You see so much more than you say. You were always quiet...always thinking. Yes, Van Helsing is why we came tonight. I need to know why they stole Sandor's body; I need to know how much they know and if they are a threat to us. And you are right, *Faust* is a dreary re-crossing of old paths. Perhaps if it were presented as an opera...."

"A musical Mephistopheles?" Elga sounded skeptical.

"Why not? If the tale can't enlighten, it could at least entertain. Perhaps your pen should be the one to set it to music."

Elga shook her head. "It's not the sort of story I'd find appealing. Besides, how many operas have been written by women?"

With thumb and forefinger Bathory took her niece by the chin, tilting her face up until Elga's gaze met her own. "You are hardly a common girl, are you? And you've had centuries to perfect your skills. Remember that piece you started to compose and played for us when we were in France, just before the Revolution? Even Carmilla was moved to tears."

"The blood stained her dress."

"Yes, well white is hardly her color, is it? But your work was magnificent; you really should finish the piece. Who would have thought Joan of Arc could be so enthralling?"

"Who would hear it?"

"There may come a day when we will no longer have to hide in the shadows. I have been looking into purchasing property in London, a city that has long forgotten many of its superstitions. We could move about there free of suspicion."

Elga's features brightened at the thought of travel. "What about the Americas?"

Bathory considered the suggestion. "Not as luxurious as London, but it would certainly put enough distance between ourselves and General Spielsdorf. I never thought he would pursue us so far from Styria. He had too much influence there, and there were too many people who remembered the old days and the old ways for us to be safe. But here the general has no political backing or official status, which gives us an advantage. This is our last line of defense; if we cannot defeat him here, we may have no other choice but to go into exile."

"Why not go away now and lose ourselves in the New World or some other remote spot? Why risk another confrontation?"

Bathory patted Elga's hand and smiled reassuringly. "Because it means spending the next few years waiting, wondering if we've really eluded Spielsdorf. After what Carmilla did to his wife and daughter, he's too determined and too dangerous. We would never rest easy until we knew he was dead."

Elga lowered her eyes, her voice growing soft. "And what of Van Helsing?

"He's a bad influence on you," Christine was saying as an attendant took she and Van Helsing's cloaks. "When you and Wellington are together, you forget I even exist. The two of you vanish for days on end, usually coming back with your pockets empty and your heads bloated with beer. And it seems to be taking you longer to recover, these days."

"Have I really been that inattentive, lately?" Van Helsing tried to look properly apologetic.

"Sometimes you seem so different from the Bram I first met and fell in love with. I almost feel like you'd *rather* spend your time with your friends at the university. Are you bored with me?"

"No, of course not. How could I be bored with..."

Christine cut him off. "Is there someone else?"

"Don't be silly. You've just said I'm with Gerald at all hours, so how could I possibly have time for a mistress?"

"Sometimes you make me feel like I'm the mistress, spending time with me only when you have a few moments to spare. It has to change, Bram. Promise to make more time for me." She squeezed his arm tightly. "Promise me."

Deep down in her eyes, Van Helsing could see the pain she had been feeling. Making it worse was the realization that, before the night was through, he would have to tell her about his suspension, as well as the journey he and Wellington were about to start. The bell sounded, announcing the performance was soon to begin, and Van Helsing took Christine by the arm to lead her up the steps to their box. Almost immediately he collided into another patron as she was about to mount the stairs.

The woman, richly dressed in a shade of blue that accented her golden tresses, had her face hidden behind her fan, but her peering eyes pierced into Van Helsing's soul and he felt sure that—should they ever meet again—he would recognize their sapphire stare. "Forgive me," he managed to stutter, repressing a shudder. "If I were to pay as much attention to where I'm going as I do to where I've been...."

"Forgive *me*," Countess Bathory insisted. "I am to blame."

Van Helsing bowed as Bathory nodded graciously, lowering her gaze as she moved past the couple.

"There are more graceful ways to make the acquaintance of a woman than to collide into her," Christine observed.

"I was momentarily blinded by your beauty."

"Oh." Christine's voice was dubious.

"Jealous?"

"No," Christine teased in droll, dry tones. "Who else could possibly have the patience to tolerate you? Besides, she's too old for some schoolboy."

"Now how do you know how old she is? Her fan hid half her face!"

Christine looked off in the direction the woman had gone. While she had given no sign of recognition, the girl felt as if she should know her. That voice and gaze reminded her of someone, possibly someone she had seen in a dream. "There was something about her eyes...the weary look you see in someone very old."

"Nonsense. There was enough of her face visible to see she's no crone. She's probably just tired, or recovering from a recent illness. I'll wager she's barely thirty.
"

"She's well past forty," Christine retorted.

"Look at her complexion; she's still full of bloom and blood. There's some bite left in her."

Christine cocked a questioning eyebrow. "I thought you said her face was half hidden?"

"You forget; I am training to be a doctor."

"There are times you certainly seem to forget it."

Van Helsing ignored her. "Observation of minute details is the greatest tool in the art of diagnosis."

"Well, you are a master of the minute, I'll give you that."

"And I admire your dancing as well." Van Helsing kissed her hand and gave her a playful twirl. "You glide across the ballroom like an angel in flight."

"I said you were a master of the minute, not the minuet."

"Any dance will do, so long as I'm dancing with you."

Neither could keep a straight face any longer, and both began to laugh. "You are beyond any hope of redemption."

"Is that why you've brought me to see *Faust*?"

The second bell sounded, and the lights in the lobby were lowered. "Quick!" Christine hissed with a quick kiss on Bram's ear. “We'll miss the opening."

Breathlessly they raced up the steps to their seats in hopes of reaching their balcony before the house lights were dimmed. Settling onto the soft, red velvet cushions of their chairs, Van Helsing looked across the audience while waiting for the curtain to go up. He heard Christine's whisper at his elbow, "How rude!"

Concerned, he turned to her. "What?"

"Those two women in the next box, do you know them?"

The lights were going down. Leaning forward to get a better look, Van Helsing was unable to see either girl's face, as they were bent close, talking animatedly amongst themselves. Yet there was something about the fair-haired woman...could she have been the one he had bumped into on the main floor? Suddenly she looked up and, as their eyes met, there seemed to be a flash of light, like he had once seen in the eyes of a wolf that had strayed close to a bonfire. The music began, and Van Helsing dismissed the moment as a trick of the theatre's light. He shook his head and said, "No, I've never seen them before. Why?"

"They were staring at you."

Bram laughed. "If they were staring, it would have been at you, wondering how anyone could look so beautiful outside of a dream."

"Aren't you the charmer?"

"No, just charmed--or should I say bewitched?--by you."

"If I thought it would keep us together, I might turn to witchcraft."

"Would you whisk me away on your broom?" Van Helsing asked.

"You need more whacking than whisking."

A sharp "Shhh!" from nearby ended any further exchange.

During the course of the play, as Van Helsing found himself toying more and more with the idea of stealing a kiss from Christine in the darkness of the theatre, a velvety voice whispered in his ear, "Be careful, someone watches you." He turned to Christine and whispered, "What?"

"I didn't say anything," she replied with a puzzled look, shaking her head.

"But you must have. I heard a voice warn me to be careful, that I was being watched."

"Sounds like your conscience is catching up with you. And while it would certainly benefit me to have you watched, I'm not likely to warn you about it, am I?"

"I thought your woman's intuition was warning you about what I was thinking."

"And what, exactly, did you have in mind, Mr. Van Helsing?"

"This." He leaned closer to kiss her.

"Bram!" she meekly protested, raising her fan to shield their faces from anyone who might look their way.

In the next box, as Bathory watched the stage, Elga watched the activity in the neighboring balcony. She was a little startled, and ashamed, at the jealousy she felt at the intimate exchange between Van Helsing and his fiancée. After all, she had no claim over him. But the pain gave way to bitterness as she realized her heart had already hoped for him. In life she would have, upon returning home, gone straight to her room and cried hot bitter tears of disappointment. But now she found herself suddenly thinking other thoughts, thoughts of hunting and hurting Van Helsing's mortal mistress, and the excitement those thoughts brought made her afraid. How easily her rival might be disposed of. But how to do it and spare him any pain?

Elga forced her feral feelings aside. It was not right; they deserved as much a chance at life, and to *live*, as she had once wanted. Unfortunately, fate had had other plans for her.

"What is it, dearest?"

Elga snapped out of her reverie at the sound of her aunt's voice. "Nothing." She could barely hear her own reply.

Bathory turned to study her niece. Taking Elga's chin in one hand, she turned the girl's face firmly toward her. Concern knitted the Countess' brow. "Are you falling in love, my child?"

Until she spoke, Elga had managed to keep her feelings in check. But, as the single word "Yes" came out, so did the tears, trickling crimson drops that burned as red-hot as their scarlet color seemed to indicate. "Aunt Elizabeth…." Unable to finish the thought, she buried her face in Bathory's bosom, sobbing silently as the tears of blood poured forth freely.

Bathory held Elga, patting her shoulder as she spoke soothingly. "Poor child, I keep forgetting you never really knew love in life; never got to walk hand-in-hand in the sunset with someone special, or share an early breakfast, basking in the warm summer sun...a sun that seemed dim compared to the glistening in a lover's eyes." She lowered her face to kiss the girl's head reassuringly. "So old, and yet still so young. You know, you *could* have him if you wanted."

Looking up, Elga shook her head fiercely. "No, not like that; not Carmilla's way. I want him to *want* me."

"I didn't mean mesmerize him or manipulate the man like a marionette; there's no satisfaction there."

"I couldn't kill her, not if it hurts him. He looks so happy with her."

Bathory laughed softly and pressed Elga closer to her. "You forget how much time is on our side. They will grow old; *she* will grow old while you remain unchanged. You could restore him, make him young again...make him one of us."

“I thought we could never become younger than we were at the time of our death?”

A sudden harshness filled Bathory’s eyes. “Who told you that? Carmilla?” Elga’s silence confirmed the countess’ suspicions.

“She’s been in the library again. The two of you must realize those books are incomplete and inaccurate. They were written by men, mortal men embracing superstition and speculation as fact. Knowledge of our nature is key to our survival; I will not have the two of you risking our safety because of some dim-witted academic’s misinformed musings.”

Although she heard Bathory’s words, Elga's attention was once more on Van Helsing and Christine. With so many conflicting thoughts and feelings flowing through her at once, her head was in a whirl. She wanted to get away from there, away from the sight of them together, so she could think. "Can we go now?"

"Yes, I think the night air would do you good."

As the two left, they passed the entrance to Van Helsing's balcony. Elga held back, pausing to peer in at the young man. Sensing a new presence near him, Van Helsing shifted in his seat to see if anyone had joined them and found Christine already looking towards the door. Following the girl's gaze, he noticed Elga in the outer corridor. As their eyes met, the vampire hurried to catch up with her aunt.

“Carmilla?” Christine whispered to herself, immediately struck by the girl’s resemblance to her new roommate.

Van Helsing turned toward her. “Who?”

Her reverie ending as she remembered the glance that had passed between the girl and Van Helsing. Christine turned on him. "Bram, who *is* she?"

"I'm sure I don't know."

Feeling bitter and betrayed, Christine left the balcony in a swirl of skirts. After a moment of indecision, Van Helsing followed in pursuit. He made his way down to the lobby, but his fiancée was nowhere in sight. He noticed a harried attendant hurried toward the exit to the street, calling out, "Mademoiselle, your wrap!" Van

Helsing dashed past him, snatching the girl's garment from the man's hand. He was only vaguely aware of the fellow's voice calling after him, "A moment, sir; your cloak!"

Standing in the middle of the street stood Christine, fists and teeth clenched. "Whore! Where are you?" As Van Helsing stepped up to quiet her, she vented her anger at him, pounding against his chest with lessening strength as she cried, "Damn it, who is she?"

Van Helsing held her close to him, partly to calm her, partly to keep her from hitting him again. "I don't know her, Chris, I swear."

"Well she knows *you*."

"What makes you say that?"

"I can feel it; I can see it in her eyes when she looks at you." Christine looked up into Van Helsing's eyes, trying to read what feelings might be there. "Is that why you were so agreeable to this evening? Is this why you didn't stand me up again tonight, to keep a rendezvous with this girl? You can't have us both, Bram."

Van Helsing looked up at the sound of an approaching carriage. Recognizing the vehicle as a cab, he hailed the driver. Looking back at Christine, her dark eyes seemed to grow even darker, as if reflecting her feelings. "So which of us will you be with tomorrow?" Her voice was calm, but cool. The horse and carriage pulled up and Van Helsing motioned for them to wait. The driver seemed to sense the strife, and touched his hat in acknowledgement.

Van Helsing felt the muscles of his jaw tighten with tension. Taking Christine by the shoulders, his grip and voice both firm. "First of all, I have *never* been with that girl. Tonight is the first time I've ever even seen her. Secondly, the only person I'm going to be with tomorrow is Gerald. We have to go to Klaus—"

The look Christine gave him was colder than the night air as she shrugged his hands from her shoulders in fury and frustration. "Maybe you're engaged to the wrong person."

"We're trying to save what little is left of our academic career here."

"I thought your mysterious expedition the other night was supposed to take care of that."

"Something went wrong."

"It always does. I mean, that's been the story of your life, hasn't it? Everything is always 'later' with you. Let me tell you something, Bram, neither of us is getting younger. *Nobody* stays young forever, especially living the life you live. We all grow older every minute of the day. Look at how many days and nights of your life you've wasted...and I've wasted mine, too, waiting on you." Christine's eyes glistened in the lamplight, shimmering from the tears she tried to fight back. In spite of the effort, she soon felt their stinging stream on her cheeks.

"Chris, things are really in a mess right now; I don't know how to begin to explain what's happened in the last two days. I'm not even sure if I understand it all, myself. Gerald and I have been suspended again, this time for the year."

Between her tears, Christine managed to laugh, until her shoulders shook as much from mirth as from her sobs. "Imagine that! You expelled? How many times does this make? You've got a brilliant brain, Bram, if only you'd learn how to use it. You've gone far, partly by cunning, partly by conning, and maybe a little by luck. If you'd spend half that energy and thought actually applying yourself, I can't begin to imagine what wonderful things you might do. There's so much talent being tossed away. It's time to grow up, my love." She kissed him gently on the cheek, then climbed into the cab. Van Helsing started to join her but she held him back, gently but firmly, with one hand.

"This is as far as we go together," Christine said. "You've spent so much of your life focused only on yourself. Almost everything you've done has been out of greed. I put up with it for a long time, because I thought it was just something you needed to get out of your system. But it doesn't get any better, it just keeps growing. The world doesn't revolve around you...or me...or anyone else. I thought, after the trouble you got into in Scotland, that once you were accepted here at Buda-Pest you'd settle down, start becoming responsible. I want a home, where there'll be someone to share my life with. I want to see my husband's face just before falling asleep; I want to wake up to the sound of his voice. I want to have children; little eyes that look up to me for love, little hands that reach out to me for guidance, voices that call to me to make the pain stop when they're sick. I'm sorry if I've wanted or expected too much from you, or made too many demands on your time; I didn't mean to love you more than you were ready to be loved. But this time it's over. I can't stand the emptiness I feel when I wake up, or the pain inside me at night, as if someone has torn my heart out. I'm tired of being alone...and I'm tired of being hurt. Goodbye, Bram."

Shutting the door behind her, Christine rapped on the ceiling of the cab, signaling the driver to move on. The vehicle lurched forward, and she buried her face in her hands.

As the cab pulled away, Van Helsing was not sure which burned him more, Christine's words or his own tears. A breeze blew the loose snow from the rooftops, and one crystalline cloud thickened, taking on a female form that hovered overhead. Unseen by the medical student, Carmilla watched as Van Helsing slowly set off on foot towards his rooms. The frozen phantom followed, silently gliding over him like an arctic angel before dissolving back into the billowing snow that drifted across the city.

Several streets away, Elizabeth Bathory stood outside her coach, well out of Van Helsing's ability to see or hear her. The conversation that had just passed between the medical student and his fiancée interested the countess as much as it had Christine, but for entirely different reasons. Joining Elga inside, she motioned for her driver to take them home.

Settling into the seat across from her niece, Bathory smiled. "They plan to go to Klausenburg." Elga looked up, puzzled. The Countess gave the girl an encouraging wink. "They're not sure what they're looking for or where to look for it, so extreme measures may not be necessary."

“And General Spielsdorf?”

“His interest in our two young friends appears limited to their encounter with Sandor, but I think we can use that interest to our advantage.”

Elga frowned, worried by her words. “You want to use the boys as bait, to lure Spielsdorf out into the open.”

The Countess nodded. “The way Spielsdorf used you.” She looked out at the darkened windows along the street as they moved through the sleeping city. Glancing slyly back to Elga, Bathory's smile broadened, showing the tips of her teeth. "I know a handsome young man in need of a nurse."

"Bra—you mean Van Helsing?"

"Yes."

"Has he been hurt?"

"Yes."

"Is it serious?"

"Yes; I've even known men to die of such an affliction." Bathory felt a touch of guilt at teasing the poor girl, especially when she noted Elga's anxiety.

Elga leaned forward, filled with fear for him, and gripped Bathory's knee tightly, oblivious to her suddenly sharpened nails. "Oh, Aunt Elizabeth, what is it? What's happened to him?"

Bathory winced as the talons tore at her dress and flesh. Elga had always worn her heart on her sleeve. Patiently pulling her niece's hand away, only to lovingly clasp it in both of her own, the countess bent close to Elga and confided, "He has a broken heart." Kissing the younger girl on the forehead, Bathory sat back in her seat. “I believe this might prove the perfect opportunity to bring Van Helsing into our little family.”

“What about his fiancée?” Elga asked.

“Carmilla may have her.”

6. A Silken Web.

It was still dark outside when Van Helsing awoke. It had been a short, restless night disturbed by dreams of the previous evening. He had said nothing of he and Christine's fight to Wellington, as his roommate had already fallen asleep before Van Helsing reached their quarters that night. Although still groggy, it was almost a relief to be up and moving about, doing anything that would keep his mind occupied.

"I was surprised to find you here last night," Van Helsing said, noticing Wellington had begun to stir. He tried to sound nonchalant as he continued to pack for the morning's trip. "I thought you'd still be with Gretchen."

"So did I," Wellington said wistfully. "Your ladylove dropped by the Wolf's Head earlier in the evening. She got to talk to Gretchen—"

"—before *you* could talk to Gretchen," Van Helsing said, finishing the thought as he took the cloak that was draped across a nearby chair and slipped it over his shoulders. Standing in front of the dressing mirror as he buttoned his collar, Van Helsing glanced at Gerald's reflection as he asked, "How bad was it?"

"Christine came in but, before she said a single word, Gretchen could tell right off something was up." Wellington paused, puzzled. "How do girls do that?"

"Beats me."

"I think that was an option they discussed. At any rate, the moment Gretchen asked her what was wrong, Chris burst into tears—where do they store all that water?—and my girl took your girl into the backroom to talk. A few minutes later, Gretchen came storming out, swearing like a sailor, and had me out the door so fast I didn't have time to grab my coat or notice the cold. What happened last night?"

Van Helsing shrugged. "I told the truth."

"How many times have I warned you about that?"

"It didn't matter, she didn't believe me." Neither spoke for a moment. Finally Van Helsing turned from the mirror to Wellington and asked, "We've had a lot of laughs over the years, haven't we?"

"More than I can remember."

"What have we got to show for it? I mean, right now, what do we have?"

Wellington thought for a moment. "Memories?"

Van Helsing shook his head. "Can we live on those? I mean, do you ever wake up in the morning and wonder, 'Why am I here? What am I going to do?'"

"No, my waking thoughts are more along the lines of 'Where am I? How did I get here, and how do I get out?'"

"No, I mean it; be serious for a moment." Van Helsing's voice was raspy as he tried to keep calm. "Why are we here? What's the point? We've spent several years together, and it *has* been fun, but we're no better off or any farther ahead than we were when we first met. Have we thrown all that time away?"

"We've certainly thrown a lot of money away."

Van Helsing laughed, quietly and bitterly, as he fell back into an armchair. Suddenly he felt very old. "You can always scrape up more money…especially if, like us, you don't let scruples get in the way. But the time, the weeks, the months, the years...we can't get the past back to gamble with again."

"You're really taking this to heart, aren't you?" Gerald leaned forward, concerned. "I really am sorry about the way things went last night. All the more reason we need to make the trip to Klausenburg and set the record straight. Look, when this is over and we've cleared our names, we'll come back, knuckle down a bit, get school over and put it all behind us."

Although his eyes were staring into the fire blazing in the hearth, Van Helsing's gaze was turned inward. "For some reason, I feel like I've started a journey where there is no coming back. I think Christine is right."

"About what?"

"A lot of things." Van Helsing stood. "It's time we were on the road; it's going to be a long day. Remember our sabers."

"What we need is a pair of pistols."

"We don't have them anymore," Van Helsing reminded him.

"If we don't, who does?"

"Morrison and Son."

"Morrison and Son?" Wellington frowned. "Who are they?"

"A pawnshop in Edinburgh." Van Helsing looked up, a weary smile tugging at one corner of his mouth. "How do you think I was able to cover that little gambling debt you racked up at The Castle Rock?"

Wellington could not believe what he was hearing. "And you never got them back?"

"You'll recall we had to leave Scotland in a hurry."

There was a soft knock at the door and then Vambery stepped into the room, a white linen envelope clutched in one hand. "I was hoping you were already up; I wanted to catch up with you before you two took off. Listen, I'm sorry about all this...."

"It's alright." Van Helsing clasped him by the shoulder. "It's really not your fault, old boy. Just look after things while we're gone, will you? We'll be back before you know it, accepting apologies from the academy all around. Who knows, we might even graduate with honors."

Vambery shook Van Helsing's hand, saying, "I'd just be happy to see the two of you graduate."

"An increasingly popular sentiment these days," Wellington observed, accepting Vambery's hand in turn.

Van Helsing handed his key to their rooms to the anatomy assistant, who turned to leave. His nostrils twitched at the faint smell he detected as Vambery passed. "A bit flowery for you, isn't it?"

Vambery was puzzled. "What do you mean?"

"That cologne...or have you just come from the arms of a woman? It's no wonder you're out and about so early...you've not been to bed yet."

"Maybe he *has* been to bed," Wellington corrected.

"Only my own...and *alone*," Vambery was quick to point out, a sheepish grin on his face. "Glad you said something, though, or I'd have forgotten this." He held up the elegant envelope he carried. "It was on the outer door of the building. Addressed to you, Bram."

Van Helsing's pulse quickened. Maybe Christine...? He was curious, but crestfallen, upon seeing his name written in a delicate but unfamiliar hand on the paper. With a dissecting scalpel that doubled for a letter opener, Van Helsing slit the note open. Taking out the piece of scented stationary, he read aloud the single sentence written on the paper, "'Take care on the road to Klausenburg.'"

"From Chris?" Wellington asked.

"No, it's not her handwriting or fragrance. Besides, I never got the chance to tell her where we were going." Puzzled, Van Helsing studied the writing intently, as if the sentence might tell him more. "This wasn't out there last night, I'm sure. Did you see anyone moving about this morning?"

"No, but then who would be out and about at this hour...." Vambery's voice trailed off as a thought came to mind.

Looking up from the note to the speaker, Van Helsing asked, "What is it?"

"There were no other tracks," Vambery replied.

"Tracks?"

"No new footprints in the snow leading up to your door."

"They've drifted over," Wellington offered.

"Yes," Van Helsing agreed. "It was still snowing when I got in."

"But the snow stopped just after midnight," Vambery pointed out, "and the depressions from two sets of boots are still visible on the walkway. Now if you were both out, that would account for those."

Wellington plucked the note from Van Helsing's hand, studying and smelling it. "Hmmm, a lady with a light step and a light hand...but a heavy heart."

Van Helsing took the note back. "What makes you say that?" For some reason, he found he did not want the letter out of his possession.

"Why else the warning?"

"What's it all mean?" Vambery asked.

"If we knew that," Wellington responded as he completed his packing, "we might be able to save ourselves a trip." He picked up a bottle of wine and started to tuck it into a bundle of clothes, then paused, biting his lower lip and mumbling.

"What is it?" asked Van Helsing.

"Breakfast."

Van Helsing looked at the bottle of wine. "I think I'll pass."

"No; I mean, had last night gone a bit smoother, Gretchen would have made us breakfast."

“We’ll be lucky if she’s still willing to lend us the horses,” Van Helsing said, “so I wouldn’t let my hopes of being stuffed *and* mounted rise too high.”

*

General Spielsdorf was sitting at the writing table of his rooms, pouring over an ancient, leather-bound volume as he ate his breakfast. He took little pleasure in eating. Food, like sleep, was merely an inconvenient necessity, taking up time that might have been spent more productively. There was a sharp rap-tap-tap at the door. "Come!" he called.

Major Arcana stepped briskly and breathlessly into the room. "The two students we've been watching, they're leaving Buda-Pest...for Klausenburg."

"What?!"

"I was at the stables checking on our horses when they came in and I overheard them talking. They're as interested in the cause of Sandor's death as we are, although for entirely different reasons. They feel they've stumbled upon a biological anomaly."

"Those young pups have no idea what they're riding into."

"Do you think Bathory has returned to Klausenburg?"

"If so, she won't be bold enough to stay at a public hotel again. The Countess can't continue to tour like a visiting dignitary, not while she knows she's being hunted. She's become a prisoner of privacy."

Arcana's eyes narrowed at the sight of the deteriorating tome in front of the general. "I've seen that book before."

Spielsdorf nodded. "It's a medieval translation of the *Scroll of Ahasver*, the oldest known work on vampirism, tracing the origins of the pestilence back to the Cult of Lilith."

"You took that from the library of Scholomance, before we burned the place to the ground."

"Bathory went there searching for the book, which tells me the information inside is important. Find Markus and get our horses ready. We're going to provide those boys with an unseen escort."

*

Although travel between Buda-Pest and Klausenburg should have been uneventful, the road was rough from the winter weather and the drifts slowly took their toll on the horses. The early darkness, coupled with the cold air, forced Van Helsing and Wellington to seek shelter, rather than ride on as they might have done on a summer's night. Stopping at a roadside inn, the two arranged for rooms and meals.

As they unpacked while waiting for supper, Van Helsing asked, "Did you get the feeling we weren't alone on the road?"

Wellington shrugged. "We passed a few people along the way, but this is hardly the tourist season."

"No, I mean...well, it was almost as if we were being followed."

"In this weather? Who would want to? Who would be able to? Even when the snow stopped, the wind was steady enough to fill in our tracks within minutes."

"Right now, the only thing I want to fill within minutes is my stomach," Van Helsing observed. "I'm so hungry I could eat a horse."

"Let's hold off on the equestrian appetizers, in case we find worse weather ahead." Wellington smiled. “If we get stranded, we may find ourselves—”

“Eating on the hoof?” Van Helsing asked, cutting him off. He shook his head wearily.

"Would you prefer horse d'oeuvres?"

"I'd prefer being horsewhipped than continuing this conversation.” Van Helsing shoved Wellington back onto his bed. “Now if you'll excuse me, I'm going to go downstairs and get something to eat." Barely were the words out of his mouth when he saw movement outside the window. Springing towards the glass, he looked outside but saw nothing.

"What is it?" Wellington asked.

"I saw a face watching us."

"Bram, we're on the second floor. And since there's no balcony...."

Van Helsing was insistent. "I tell you there was somebody there."

"Maybe it was just your reflection." Wellington's voice sounded doubtful.

"Or my imagination?" Van Helsing added for him.

"Well, you haven't really been yourself since you and Chris.... Look, I know you're hurt, but if you really want her back, maybe you can—"

"Maybe I can't!" Van Helsing snapped. "What then?"

"Then maybe it wasn't meant to be; maybe you'll meet someone else."

"Maybe I don't want someone else. And maybe I really don't want to talk about this. If you know it bothers me, then why are we even having this conversation?"

Wellington started to speak but hesitated. Turning to leave, he paused, thought for a moment, and then said, "You're right, I shouldn't have brought it up. I guess I'm just not used to seeing you like this. I wanted this trip to be an adventure, to be fun, to be like things used to be."

“We can’t keep living in the past. Things change, and we have to change, too…including our priorities.”

Wellington’s mouth curved into a wistful smile, and the expression was mirrored in his eyes. “So you don’t fancy us spending the rest of our lives at university?”

Van Helsing returned the smile. “Only if we become professors.”

“Lord, no!” Wellington shuddered at the thought. “We’d only end up with younger versions of ourselves for students.”

Although he suddenly found himself with little appetite after the spat, Van Helsing forced himself to go down to supper with Wellington. At least he might find the wine a suitable soporific. He knew the tension he felt inside would keep conversation at a minimum, but he knew it would pass by morning. The two men had known each other long enough to make allowances for one another, and "sorry" was no longer necessary.

As Van Helsing picked at his plate, he noticed Wellington staring at three soldiers who had just come in and were warming themselves by the fire. Dressed in military garb, they kept their backs to the rest of the room, and spoke in quick, quiet tones, occasionally stealing looks over their shoulders at the few customers in the place. Yet, as Van Helsing began to study them, he noticed they often cast their gaze at he and Wellington’s table. Finally he asked, "Friends of yours?"

“I don’t remember seeing any of them before,” Wellington said. “Their uniforms aren’t familiar.”

“I know those markings,” Van Helsing said, trying not to be obvious as he studied the soldiers. “They’re from Klausenburg.”

The door burst open, as if thrown back by a strong hand, but the doorway stood empty. Then a dark, misty form appeared out of the hazy winter night, a woman in a hooded cloak of forest green, with the lower half of her face muffled to protect it from the wind. She stood motionless at the threshold, her dark eyes searching the room until they met, and held, Van Helsing's gaze.

As she looked at the student, he found the surrounding sounds of the room were drowned out by a strange silence, and that everything seemed out of focus except for her unblinking eyes. He was vaguely aware that there was recognition in her expression, and even a brief moment of happiness. Something in the back of his mind told him they had met before, yet he could not remember when or where. Neither of them looked away, nor did there seem to be a sense of self-consciousness. Slowly standing, Van Helsing smiled and motioned her forward with the invitation, "Won't you join us? You'll catch your death out on a night like this."

A look of amusement, and a touch of sadness, greeted his remark. She stepped forward as the wind blew the door closed behind her and was about to speak when the proprietor's wife, an elderly woman who had been serving their patrons, dropped a tray of tankards. Shaking her head in horror, she crossed herself. The girl's eyes seemed to flicker at the gesture, as if a flame burned behind them. As the newcomer turned on the poor woman, the owner came out from behind the bar, putting his arm protectively about her. "Please," he pleaded, his eyes wild with fear, "my wife meant no offense!"

Before the girl in the green cloak could answer, the three officers who had been standing at the fire had moved quickly between her and the door, sabers drawn. Whirling at the sounds of the soldiers, the cloaked figure confronted them, her head held high as she addressed one of the officers. "Tell me, General, can you afford to make the same mistake twice?"

General Spielsdorf glared at Elga, and for a moment neither moved, as if each were waiting for the other to let their guard down. With a grim smile, Spielsdorf nodded his head and, stepping aside to open the door, spoke softly, "Good night, Countess. Please remember me to your aunt."

Elga curtsied in response to the courtesy and, in a velvet voice, replied, "Of course, Herr General; we look forward to having you for dinner one evening." With a delicate laugh, she slipped past the officer and into the night. Quickly settling their account with the landlord, Spielsdorf, Arcana and Markus dashed out the door in pursuit.

"How odd," Van Helsing commented.

"Well, soldiers are known for chasing women." Wellington returned to his meal. "The lady seemed quite interested in you, though. Do you know her?"

"I don't think so…yet there *was* something familiar about her, as if she had come from some forgotten dream." Van Helsing grew thoughtful. "Is that possible?"

"To dream about someone you've never met, only to find they really do exist?" Shrugging, Wellington pushed his plate away. "Who knows? The mind remains a mystery. We've both dissected brains but, unlike the rest of the body, there are no apparent internal organs inside to assign individual functions. If there is a 'dream gland,' then it's time to let it get some exercise. I'm warm and well fed, now it's off to bed."

*

Frustration and exhaustion made what sleep there was for Van Helsing fitful and feverish. Drifting in and out of consciousness, he could hear Christine's final words to him echo over and over in his mind, leaving his heart feeling haunted and hollow. This dark despair found his dreams turning to nightmares, each more gothic and grotesque than before. In one nocturnal vision he found himself in a chapel, waiting for Christine. There was the soft rustle of skirts and he turned to see her coming down the aisle toward him in a wedding gown, her long, dark hair forming a formal contrast against the white dress and veil. As she neared Van Helsing, her dress took on the crimson color of the light seeping through the scarlet panes of stained glass above the altar.

When Christine reached him, she slipped her arms gently about Van Helsing, drawing him near. "Do you really love me?" Her voice was as soft as a sigh.

"Yes," Van Helsing replied, kissing her through the veil.

"Forever?"

"'Til death do us part,'" he whispered. Van Helsing lifted the veil to kiss her again, only to reveal a grinning skull where the girl's face should have been, a hellish light blazing in the eye sockets. With a scream, Van Helsing tore himself away from the apparition. He was still screaming when he awoke in his bed, shivering in sweat-drenched sheets.

*

In spite of little real sleep, Van Helsing and Wellington were up for a dawn breakfast, hoping an early start would help them gain time on the wind-swept roads. While the plan seemed sound at the time, the duo found the weather growing worse as they got closer to Klausenburg. The iron-grey sky grew dark as evening once more threatened to engulf them.

Van Helsing brought his horse to a stop. He looked about at the woods and fields, trying not to think of the thick clouds rolling overhead, hoping for some recognizable landmark. "Klausenburg has to be here. We should almost be on top of it."

"What if we're not?" asked Wellington. "What then? I don't see a convenient inn."

"Surely we can come up with some kind of shelter." Van Helsing motioned towards some branches torn from the mist-entwined trees by the winter storm. "If we can build a fire...."

"Speaking of fire," Wellington pointed down the road, "do you see that?"

Van Helsing leaned forward in his saddle, straining to get a better look. In the distance, dim lights twinkled in the twilight, faint flickering flames that almost seemed like fiery eyes watching them. "What is it?"

"In this weather, so long as it's burning, it doesn't matter." Wellington urged his horse onward.

Van Helsing gave a weary smile before setting off after his comrade. "Much as I hate to admit it, you might be right."

Nearing the source of the lights, Van Helsing and Wellington could make out large shadowy forms in the fog ahead, pale at first, but growing darker and more solid as they closed the gap between themselves and their destination. Drawing closer, they realized the great hulking mass was an ornate stone bridge, a relic of another century. Hanging half off the ancient edifice, whose stones were worn away by weather and age, was a grand carriage as black as the night itself. It was the golden glow of the vehicle's lamps that had been the fierce pinpoints of light beckoning them. The coach had apparently lost control on the ice, and now teetered dangerously between road and river. Only the straining efforts of the team of horses, themselves as dark as the vehicle they pulled, kept the carriage from plunging into the icy waters below.

As the two companions reached the edge of the bridge, they saw a single footman assessing the situation while the driver tried to coax his horses forward. At the sound of approaching hoofbeats, the footman looked up and smiled in relief. Addressing them in German, the servant said, "Thank heaven you've come along. Could you aid my mistress? The horses lost their footing on the ice when we attempted to cross the bridge. We nearly went over the side."

Drawing his horse up closer to the carriage, Wellington found himself struggling to keep the beast in check as it neared the vehicle. The creature pawed at the ground with one hoof and snorted nervously. Recalling the old adage about animals sensing danger, he dismissed the horse's behavior and rubbed its neck reassuringly.

"Looks like ice is all that's still holding these stones together," Van Helsing observed. He glanced over one side of the bridge. Both banks of the river were edged with ice, like frozen ribbons along the shore. "I wouldn't want to feel the icy embrace of those waters." Turning his mount around, he looked at his traveling companion and cocked an eyebrow. "Ready to do your good deed for the week?"

Wellington looked at Van Helsing with mock injury. "Have I ever been known to say no to a lady."

"I wasn't aware you had ever been with a *lady*." Van Helsing swung down from his saddle. "If we could rig ropes to the carriage, and use our own horses to pull it back onto more solid stone...."

"...then guide it across what's left of the bridge and on to the road on the other side." Wellington nodded in agreement.

The footman went to get the ropes required from the coach's tackle, and Van Helsing called to the shadowy figure who peered out from the darkened coach window, "A moment Madame, and we shall have you on your way once more."

The ropes and horses were soon in place, and the two friends began to ease the back of the carriage up onto the bridge with their mounts while the driver and footman used the coach's horses to keep the front of the vehicle from veering off the solid surface. After several minutes of slipping, sweating and swearing, the vehicle was safely centered on the bridge. Only then did Van Helsing notice the great golden "B" embossed on the back of the carriage. Although he did not recognize the dragon crest on the coach door, the vehicle apparently belonged to a person of great importance. Wellington motioned for the driver to continue crossing, while he and Van Helsing followed close behind in case of further mishap.

Once they were safely on the other side, a woman's voice from within the coach spoke sharply in a strange tongue to the driver, who brought the horses to a halt. The voice spoke again, this time more softly, and in German, "Two gallant souls, coming to the aid of a stranger. It would seem there is still honor in the hearts of at least some men in this part of the world." There was a pause, then she continued, this time in English, "But in spite of the language you speak, your accents tell me you are not from this part of the world. Come closer, and let me see the faces of my friends."

As they approached, a dim light appeared inside the carriage, silhouetting the speaker in the window.

"She speaks English," Wellington said, somewhat surprised.

"French as well," the woman replied in that language with a laugh, delighted at the impression she made. The lights within the carriage blazed up, filling the interior with a warm golden glow. Silently the door swung open. "Come, my cavaliers, and enjoy the comfort of my coach!"

As the two men accepted the hospitality of their host, they discovered she was not alone but traveled with a young lady who, by her appearance, was not quite their own age. The one who had spoken to them had blue eyes that, when their gaze met, made Van Helsing feel as if she were staring into his soul. Her hair was pulled to one side, where it ran across the front of her cloak like a waterfall tinted gold by the early morning sun, and her lips had the color and richness of a deep red wine. For a moment, Van Helsing found himself trying to imagine what it would feel like, taste like, to kiss those lips, and was shocked to find that he was leaning towards her.

"Are you well?" the woman asked. "You seem weary."

Van Helsing straightened in his seat. "Yes, thank you. I...." his voice trailed off.

"We've been on the road for quite some time, and I fear the weather has taken its toll on us," Wellington explained. "Tell me, are we close to Klausenburg...?" He, too, failed to finish his sentence, suddenly realizing he was not sure how to address the lady of such carriage.

Sensing his plight, she gave Wellington a comforting smile. "After all you have done for me, you must think me ill-mannered, indeed, to have not introduced myself earlier. I am Countess Bathory and this," she indicated the other girl, "is my niece, Lady Elga, Countess Dolingen of Gratz.

Until that moment Van Helsing had only taken partial notice of the coach's other occupant, as Bathory had such a commanding presence. But, at the mention of her name, his attention was reflexively drawn to Elga. He caught the hint of a faint but familiar fragrance, almost identical to the scent on the unsigned note that arrived at their rooms before they left Buda-Pest. Why did she look so familiar? Her face was framed by auburn hair, and on either side of her aquiline nose were moist dark eyes that seemed to burn red in the flickering lamplight. Or did the fire come from within? Van Helsing guessed her to be but a few years younger than himself. He suddenly realized he had been staring when Elga, who had held his gaze with the same mesmerizing intensity of her aunt, looked down and smiled demurely to herself. Although her eyes were now directed elsewhere, Van Helsing felt as if she were still watching him.

Following Bathory's example, Wellington continued the introductions. "Gerald Wellington, at your service, Countess."

"You have been service enough, already, friend Gerald, for which my niece and I are both grateful. And does your friend have a name?"

"My fellow student and roommate, Abraham Van Helsing."

"Well," smiled the Countess, "now that we are all old acquaintances, allow me to answer your question: Klausenburg is not far from this place, but the hour and weather make travel difficult. You must accept the hospitality of my home, safe from the dangers of the night."

"There is danger in the night," Van Helsing responded. "Which is why we are out at such an hour. A man named Sandor was killed near here just a few days ago. Perhaps you have heard of the incident?"

Elga seemed agitated at his words. Putting a comforting arm about the girl, Bathory breathlessly pleaded, "Now I must insist that you accompany us, not only out of gratitude, but out of concern for our safety on the road. Please, do not deny me; we are strangers here, and have no one to turn to. We have only recently moved to this country, from my ancestral home near Styria, and are the last of our household to arrive. Most of the servants were sent on ahead with our possessions in order to make ready for us."

"How could we refuse such a request?" Wellington placed a comforting hand over the clasped hands of Bathory and her niece.

Bathory smiled, and there was something almost cat-like in her expression. "Then take to your beasts and follow us. It is but a short distance from here."

Leaving the carriage, the two friends remounted their horses. As the vehicle pulled away, the lights within dimmed, but not before Van Helsing caught a glimpse of Elga watching him intently. With rekindled spirits, they set off after the coach. But happier hearts did not muddy their memories of why they had come, and so it was with hands on the hilts of their swords that they brought up the rear for fear of death in the darkness.

Wellington gave Van Helsing a reassuring wink. “Bram, I do think Lady Luck is finally smiling on us.”

Van Helsing shook his head with good-natured tolerance, knowing his companion was already imagining food and drink by a cheerful hearth upon arriving at Bathory's estate. "Lady Luck? I would have said guardian angels."

"Then I look forward to the gentle caress of their wings."

7. Sanguine Sanctorum.

No sooner had the entourage set off for Bathory's manor when the snow began to lessen. The wind died down as the thick wet flakes grew fewer and fewer, and the clouds overhead parted to reveal the moon, which bathed the landscape in its pale white light. The area they traveled through was full of jagged hills and trees, which appeared as dark blotches against the wintry blanket covering the land.

Riding close behind the Countess' carriage, Van Helsing and Wellington briefly found themselves plunged back into darkness as twisted trees formed a canopy over the road with their dense limbs, leaving only the quivering flames of the lamps on the coach as a guide. The driver seemed to know this part of the country well, as he took the road with amazing swiftness. Finally, off in the distance, a large darkened estate could be seen jutting against the night sky and the two companions wondered if this was their destination. As if in answer, lights began appearing at the windows of the silhouetted chateau.

Nearing the ancient edifice, Van Helsing suddenly felt his heart racing, his pulse throbbing throughout his body with every beat. The hair on his forehead and at the base of his neck grew moist, not just with snow and mist, but sweat as well. The entire area was heavily wooded and wild, and the howl of wolves could be heard in the distance. They were close enough now that the house could be seen in more detail in the soft moonlight. A massive stone wall with heavy iron gates extended across the front of the manor and continued on around the building, disappearing into the darkness. The grounds of the estate seemed almost an extension of the forest, unkempt and overgrown after years of abandonment.

As the coach approached the gate, the driver whipped up the horses and their hooves tore into the snow and gravel of the drive. Just as it seemed beast and barrier would collide, the gates were thrown back and the carriage raced inside. Urging their horses onward, the riders saw no trace of servants at the gate, yet the sounds of the gates slamming shut behind them and the lock groaning from years of misuse echoed in their ears. The coach still showed no signs of slowing, and the two students were surprised to see a glistening crescent of silver directly ahead of them.

"A moat," Van Helsing thought aloud as they crossed the stone bridge that led over the frozen water, the icy surface reflecting the moonlight like a mirror. In places, partially sunken chunks of stone protruded through the ice like jagged teeth. These fractures, some apparently part of a series of arches, appeared to be sections of an ancient foundation, left unrepaired and unremoved by the previous owners.

Reaching the other side of the bridge, the carriage slowed as it passed under an enormous, ornately-carved arch and entered the castle courtyard. There, a lone servant stood waiting, torch in hand, at the entrance to the manor house. On either side of the massive wooden doors, braziers blazed to light the steps leading up to the entrance. As if their arrival were a signal, the snowstorm began again, wind whipping violently about the party, and groaning as it poured through the nooks and crannies of the ancient stone walls.

"It's breathtaking," Van Helsing exclaimed as he brought his horse to a halt. He looked about, but could see only sections of the estate, briefly thrown in sharp relief by dying shafts of moonlight unsuccessfully trying to struggle through the quickly closing clouds.

"The grounds cover a vast area," Bathory replied with no slight pride, having heard his comment as she alighted from her coach. "The woods seem to stretch out forever; even on horseback I have yet to reach the edge of the estate. Deep in the forest still stand the remains of an ancient church and burial vault...a convenience for those of other times."

Wellington and Van Helsing began to undo their belongings from their mounts, but Bathory held up one hand. "Leave them; my people will look after your horses and luggage. Come inside and enjoy the warmth of food and fire."

Van Helsing patted his horse on the neck as a groomsman took the reins. Turning to go up the steps, he was surprised to find Elga behind him, as he had not yet seen her step down from the carriage. There was a hesitant smile as she slipped past him, saying, "Follow me."

The party, led by Elga and Bathory, entered the manor, let in by a figure that lingered in the shadows as if fearing to be seen. Stepping across the threshold, Van Helsing found himself unable to move at the sight before him. At the end of the long hall were twin staircases of marble, which curved up into the darkness of the next level. Between the two sets of steps was an enormous fireplace, the roar of its blazing logs adding an eerie touch to the hellish glow the flames created. This wildly waltzing light, the only illumination in the great hall, cast long shadows across the floor from the trunks and crates that littered the place.

"I must apologize for the condition of the grounds and estate, but we have had to move under less than ideal circumstances and have not yet had the opportunity to make the place more presentable," Bathory explained. "Many of the fixtures are no longer useable, and so light is limited. As you could see from the outside, some sections have fallen into neglect and disrepair, and are dangerous. Should you find any doors locked or closed to you, it is out of concern for your safety, and not because you are unwelcome." Bathory excused herself for a moment, and vanished through a shadowy doorway, leaving Elga near the fireplace to watch over their guests.

"You know," Wellington mused in low tones to Van Helsing, "we *could* offer to help them unpack and get settled in."

"What about the Sandor investigation?" Van Helsing asked.

"With that wind outside, I doubt we'll make much progress tomorrow; the roads will be drifted shut. If it keeps up all night, it may be days before we can even attempt to leave. Time and weather may have already wiped away any traces of what we're looking for."

"But it won't wipe away who did the deed."

"But it will limit their ability to travel just as it limits ours…unless they've already left the area." Wellington rubbed the back of his aching neck. The idea of staying there seemed very inviting at the moment. A sudden lethargy seemed to have seized him upon entering the hall.

Van Helsing began to undo his cloak. "It seems as if our tenure at Buda-Pest is tenuous at best." He looked about the hallway as he approached the hearth, his attention eventually drawn to the canopy of cobwebs covering the cathedral ceiling. Maybe it was the long journey, or maybe it was the prolonged exposure to the weather, but the warmth of the blaze made the cares of the day melt away. "I don't know what sort of resources the Countess has, but it's going to take some doing to restore this place."

"Resources? Did you see that carriage and those clothes?" Gerald's tone was incredulous. "They can probably afford an army of architects."

"If the Sandor case does turn out to be a dead end, we're going to have a considerable amount of spare time on our hands," Van Helsing mused. Maybe we'll have better luck as masons than we did with medicine. There's certainly enough work to be done here to last a lifetime."

Countess Bathory, accompanied by an anemic-looking maid, returned with a candelabrum in her hand. Smiling, Bathory motioned for the two friends to come forward, saying, "I should think you'll want to get out of those wet clothes before you take cold. Your luggage has already been attended to. Ilona"—Bathory gestured to the servant girl whose fair hair almost matched her pale complexion—"will show you to your rooms. I have had brandy sent up to help warm the blood on a such a night, but if there is something else you prefer...."

"You've been most generous, Countess," Van Helsing reassured her.

"I still consider myself in your debt; had you not come along, my niece and I might still be on that bridge. We have already supped, but I shall see to it you are provided with food shortly." Bathory handed Ilona the candelabrum and stepped aside. With a bow to her mistress, the servant turned to lead the way up the sweeping steps, pausing to look over her shoulder to make sure the two friends followed.

At the foot of the staircase Van Helsing started to bid their host good night, only to find both Bathory and Elga were gone. Frowning, he quickly caught up with Ilona and Wellington, not wanting to drown in the darkness should the flickering light of the candles get too far ahead of him. As they followed the stairs around, Van Helsing discovered that it joined with the other set of steps in a landing, from which rose a smaller staircase that covered the remaining distance to the next floor. Upon reaching the landing, Van Helsing found himself confronted by the familiar face of a young lady peering down at him from a large portrait that hung on the wall.

Although Ilona and Wellington seemed to take little notice of the painting, Van Helsing held back to look at it while the light lasted. The image startled him, for the girl in the portrait, although dressed in the manner of a different age, had the same dark piercing eyes and high noble nose as Elga. Even the hair, while worn different, was identical in color. The lips, like those of the Countess and her niece, were a rich velvet red. In spite of this, there was a distinct individuality about the girl that made Van Helsing sense it that it was not Elga.

Noticing Van Helsing's hesitation, Ilona stopped on the steps. "Is there anything the matter, sir?"

Wellington started to come back down. "What is it, Bram?"

"This picture...the girl in it looks like...." Van Helsing's voice trailed off. In the gloom the portrait appeared to have changed expressions, the corners of the mouth slightly curved into a faint smile he was sure had not been there before. And the eyes, which Van Helsing was certain had been looking off to one side, were looking at him now, holding his gaze and searching his soul.

Ilona looked off into the darkness, listening to something in the distance. With a slight nod of her head, as if in answer to an unspoken command, she turned to Van Helsing and said, "If you would like to stay behind to study the portrait, I could light the candles here on the landing for you."

"Thank you." Van Helsing smiled. "I *would* like that...very much."

"Falling in love with a picture?" Wellington asked as the servant attended to the candles. "I didn't realize you were such a romantic."

The candles on either side of the portrait lit, Ilona curtsied before leading Wellington away to his chambers. In a silent reverie that almost bordered upon enchantment, Van Helsing continued to gaze at the painting. His attention intently focused on the face, he was startled by the sudden appearance of Elga, who now stood silently beside him.

"I'm sorry; I didn't meant to frighten you." Elga smiled, a touch self-consciously Van Helsing thought, as she seemed careful to cover her mouth as she did so. Although she avoided looking at him, there was a feeling of warmth, and a desire to be liked, that seemed to emanate from her.

Looking from the girl beside him to the girl in the portrait, Van Helsing decided to confirm his suspicions. "This...isn't you, is it?"

Elga shook her head. "That is my cousin Carmilla, the Countess Karnstein." Van Helsing frowned at the name. Why did it sound familiar? Before he could ponder the problem, Elga spoke again. "Some people mistake us for twins because of the resemblance." Again came the smile, one hand discreetly covering the mouth. Looking up at the portrait, Elga added, "She may join us later; she's been rather ill lately."

"She is beautiful," Van Helsing observed. Elga looked down, distressed by the interest he showed in the picture. "But," he continued, covering any unintentional slight he may have made in teasing her, "only because she reminds me of her cousin, Countess Dolingen...or do you prefer to be called Lady Elga?"

Looking up, her dark eyes shining with delight at the compliment, she quickly, yet gently, reached up and kissed him on the check. The joy spread quickly across her face, and her smile partially revealed her lustrous teeth, the canines of which were sharper and more developed than normal. "Just Elga," she corrected him. Suddenly aware of her reaction, she grew embarrassed and drew back slightly. "You must be very tired; you've been on the road all day. Your room is up here." She reached up and removed a candle from beside the portrait. Without another word she moved quickly up the steps and Van Helsing followed her.

Elga led Van Helsing down a corridor, which branched off into two directions. Indicating the west passage, she commented, "Your friend is in the first room to the left." Then, motioning to the east with the candle, she guided him to a door at the end of that passageway. "I'm sorry we couldn't arrange for your rooms to be together, but there is still so much to be done here, and with only a few servants...."

"I may not be there with him, but I am here with *you.* I have no complaints about the accommodations." Even by candlelight Van Helsing could see her blush at the compliment. Elga placed one hand on his shoulder and started to speak, then changed her mind. "No need to be shy," Van Helsing reassured her. "Especially under your own roof. What were you going to ask?"

"Did you mean it?" Elga's eyes searched his.

"Mean what?" He smiled at her hesitation.

Elga lowered her eyes, her long, dark lashes hiding whatever expression had been there. "What you said back at the portrait of Carmilla."

"Don't you know how pretty you are?" Van Helsing gently lifted her chin. "When I get to Klausenburg, remind me to buy you a mirror."

Elga whirled and fled into the darkness.

"Women," sighed Van Helsing. "The more I learn, the less I know." Fumbling for the latch, he stepped into his room, and found a friendly fire on the hearth. His bags had been unpacked and his things carefully laid out upon the dresser. Sitting on a side table, twinkling in the firelight, was the promised decanter and a plate of cheese and meat. Warmed inside and out by the brandy and the blaze, he soon fell into a contented sleep.

*

It was nearly noon when Van Helsing awoke, although he was not immediately aware of the hour. Still only semi-conscious, he had the impression someone was leaning over him, as if to whisper in his ear. Suddenly all sleep was gone, and he turned over in the bed, eyes wide open and every sense on edge. He was alone.

Dismissing it as a dream, Van Helsing sat upright and rubbed his aching neck. He must have slept with his head turned at an odd angle. It was only then that he was aware of the faint smell of perfume. Checking his watch, which rested on the nightstand beside the bed, he was alarmed to note how much of the day was already gone and quickly got dressed.

Out in the corridor, mournful shafts of grey winter light seeped into the murky hallway from the windows. Van Helsing found himself trying to remember which direction he had come from the night before. Somewhere in the estate a clock chimed twelve. As the last bell faded away Van Helsing realized Elga was standing nearby, her back to him as she gazed through the frozen panes of glass at the courtyard below. His eyes must have taken a few moments to get adjusted to the gloom, as he would have sworn the corridor was empty when he first stepped into it. Elga seemed to sense his presence and turned to greet him, her face lighting up at the sight of him. As she smiled, the light in the corridor seemed a bit brighter to Bram, a notion he quickly dismissed.

"Did you sleep well?" Elga asked, taking a step toward him.

"Too well, it would seem." Van Helsing let her lead him down the passageway, not wanting to admit to feeling lost. "You'll think me the most lazy fellow that ever lived, getting up at this hour."

"I've risen later." Although unnoticed by Van Helsing, Elga glanced sideways at the student, a mischievous gleam in her eye, as if at some private joke.

"You’re different than any other girl I've ever met." Van Helsing noticed Elga’s questioning look and added, “It's hard to believe someone your age is already a countess."

"I'm older than I look." Elga's reply seemed more amused than defensive.

Van Helsing stopped, and studied Elga with mock sobriety. He began prodding her face as if he were a physician preparing a diagnosis, turning her head at different angles and making reproachful noises. Elga good-naturedly put up with the "examination," curious as to its outcome. Gently using his forefinger to pull at one of her eyelids, Van Helsing bent closer to minutely study the eye in question, and felt Elga grow tense as his face stopped just inches from hers. "You're right," he conceded, "almost an old maid."

With a sudden fury, Elga knocked his hand away. "You needn't be mean to me!" Van Helsing was amazed at the strength behind the blow. Before he could recover she had turned away. Ashamed at her anger, she apologized. "I...I didn't mean to strike you. That was rude."

Van Helsing could tell by her voice Elga was near to tears. "I'm the one who was rude." Reaching into his pocket, he offered her his handkerchief. Without turning around, she accepted it. "I shouldn't have teased you. Forgive me?"

Elga nodded, wiping her eyes. "Will you forgive *me*?"

"Then we're still friends?"

Elga turned and searched Van Helsing's face, her eyes burning into his as if searching his soul. As he started to move forward she quickly did the same, slipping her arms about him and hugging him close, her face pressed to his chest. Once more Van Helsing found himself surprised at the power she possessed at her embrace. "I'm not very good with people," she explained, then realized how intimate their position was. Reluctantly, she pulled away. "I guess I never have been. Maybe that's why I was always passed over for Carmilla."

"Here," Van Helsing held out his hand for his handkerchief. "I promise I'll never give you cause to need that again."

"No, not now!" Elga took a step back, clutching the cloth closer to her for fear he would see the bloody traces of her tears. "I'll have it cleaned and returned to you."

"They're only tears. I'm sure your staff have more pressing things to tend to than my laundry." Van Helsing shook his head. "I guess I'm not used to having my every need and whim looked after. The independence your status gives you…endless days to pursue all your inspirations and passions."

"Too much time is not a blessing," Elga said. "Sometimes it can be very lonely."

"But surely, between Countess Bathory and your cousin Carmilla, there's always someone to talk to." Van Helsing gave her a playful wink. "And I'm sure you've attended several balls and schools over the years. Why, in your position, you must have met dozens of people."

"Most of the people I knew are…" Elga paused, as if catching herself, "…gone."

"That will change soon enough; you've just moved here and haven't had a chance to meet anyone yet."

Elga smiled. "I've met you."

"It'll get better," Van Helsing reassured her.

"I have a request."

"I could hardly refuse the command of countess," Van Helsing replied.

There was a wistful expression in Elga's eyes that, for a moment, made her seem suddenly older. "Could I call you 'Bram,' like your friends do?"

"You don't ask for much, do you?"

"The less you ask for, the less disappointment you have to deal with," Elga said with a slight shrug.

"A practical, but somewhat melancholy, philosophy," Van Helsing observed.

"Sometimes I wish I were more like Carmilla; she's so passionate about everything."

"What are you passionate about?"

There was a pause before Elga spoke, reminding Van Helsing of a shy little girl who has just been asked her name. "I have my music."

"Then I must have a command performance," Van Helsing insisted. "I haven't heard music since…." His voice trailed off as he remembered that last night with Christine at the theatre, and his features darkened.

"I seem to have lost you," Elga said. "Who were you thinking of just then?"

"No one," Van Helsing replied, trying to sound nonchalant.

"Don't be afraid to tell me." Van Helsing was not sure if Elga had actually spoken the words, or if he had only imagined hearing her voice inside his head. "You should never feel fear when you're with me."

Van Helsing felt light-headed. What had happened at the theatre? For a moment there had been someone else there with them during the play, a girl with dark eyes that watched them from the shadows. Had Christine called her "Carmilla?" He could still see those dark eyes, but could not remember the girl's face. Looking at Elga, he again saw those eyes, still watching him. "You…?"

“What is it, Bram?” The sound of Elga’s voice suddenly broke his reverie.

Van Helsing looked around, confused. What had they been talking about? Finally he spoke a single word, “*Faust*.”

“*Faust*?” Elga frowned.

“I was just saying that the last time I heard music was at a performance of *Faust*.”

The look of worry passed from Elga’s face. “For a moment I thought you had found something sinister about me.”

“No, nothing *diabolique*.” Van Helsing smiled, taking Elga by the elbow to lead her down the corridor. “Only angelic.”

As Van Helsing and Elga exchanged pleasantries, Wellington was enjoying the late breakfast laid out for him in the dining room. No servants were about, nor had he seen any sign of Countess Bathory. However a starving stomach had little need of encouragement and, with the practical concern of the food growing cold (or, even worse, going to waste), the student was determined not to disappoint his host. In his mind, it was his duty as the best of guests to do the meal justice.

Between mouthfuls, Wellington checked his pocket watch against the marble clock on the mantle, making sure his timepiece was merely not in error. "I *did* sleep in."

“Perhaps this will help,” came a voice at his side. Startled, Wellington looked up as Ilona set a cup of strong black coffee before him. The aroma drifted up to his nostrils with a warmth that quickly drifted down into his throat. She nodded in greeting, and then placed a silver coffee pot on the table.

Wellington gratefully swept up the cup, pausing long enough to say, "Good morning, Ilona; I didn't hear you come in," before sipping the dark brew.

"I'm told I have a light step." Ilona stood there, her arms down and her hands folded before her as she waited to see if he would need anything else. The slight pulse of his throat as he swallowed his coffee caught her eye and she watched the movement with catlike curiosity.

Gradually growing aware of Ilona's stare, Wellington was surprised to find himself uneasy at the attention the girl showed him. Only when he spoke did she met his gaze. "I suppose breakfast at midday *is* a bit out of the ordinary; not quite in keeping with Franklin's 'Early to bed, early to rise.'" Wellington paused, and then added, "I guess that's why I'm not healthy, wealthy and wise. Still, though, two out of three's not bad."

Ilona smiled at the comment, but there was something harsh in the expression. "Given the conditions of the road and the hours you must have traveled, Countess Bathory anticipated you and your companion would rise late."

Wellington laughed. "Well if the Countess is not surprised, then I am not ashamed…except at having inconvenienced you by interrupting your routine."

"Will there be anything else, sir?" Ilona's eyes moved again to Wellington's throat. "Is there something I can get you…anything I can do….?"

Before Wellington could answer, a large moth flitted past his face. The sudden appearance of the insect seemed to upset Ilona, who took an involuntary step away from the student. Oblivious to her distress, he attempted to swat at the creature but it darted out of reach. After silently circling about the table, the moth flew off through a nearby archway.

The winged intruder gone, Wellington again returned his attention to his breakfast. “I'm going to miss this when we leave.”

"I will not permit it," came an authoritative voice from the arch where the moth had vanished. Countess Bathory greeted him with a smile, yet there was a firmness underlying the expression. "My apologies if it seems I am ordering you about; I fear I still consider myself elsewhere, where my word is law. But you have come a long way, and should rest. The weather is not so friendly to the traveler this time of year and the cold is hard on the heart. You will find the road this morning even more impassable than last night.” Wellington suddenly realized Ilona had disappeared from the dining room, but he had not seen or heard her depart. He was unable to give the matter much thought as the Countess continued her conversation. “It has been a long time since I have had the opportunity to entertain guests. The chateau we last lived in was not easily accessible; travel through the mountains was treacherous, what with wolves, bandits and ill-kept roads. Already I can see a change in Elga from your visit. I, too, feel renewed from the sight of fresh faces. Young blood is what this place needs to make it come alive again. I insist you remain with us for a while longer, until the climate is more hospitable."

Wellington protested politely. "But who knows how long or how severe...."

"Your presence will hardly inconvenience us in a house this size." Bathory joined Wellington at the table, allowing him to pull out the chair for her. "And we have provisions enough to provide for any want you may have. Is your business in Klausenburg really so pressing? I am not without influence in that area, and may be of some service to you...." She let her voice trail off, indicating that she wished to hear more of his plans.

Wellington was momentarily at a loss for words. How could he delicately explain the purpose behind his trip? Finally, he spoke. "Bram and I are students at the university in Buda-Pest. Or, rather, we *were* students there. We were examining what can only be described as a medical mystery."

"Ah," Bathory beamed, "you have a thirst for knowledge. Excellent! You can never tell where the path you pursue may lead. Tell me more."

"It's a strange story. You may recall last evening Bram mentioned there had been a murder on the road near here? The victim's name was Sandor and, in spite of receiving what should have been fatal wounds, he did not die."

"No, he did not die." A fleeting smile seemed to steal across the Countess' face, but the student dismissed it as a trick of light and shadow as Bathory added, "Sandor was a most unfortunate fellow."

"Then you *knew* him?" Wellington was amazed.

Bathory bit her lower lip before replying, choosing her words carefully. "I had dealings with him. He was subject to cataleptic comas, as I believe your men of science call them."

"But his wounds, those were the work of an attack."

"I have no doubt he was ambushed. Possibly the shock sent him into such a somnambulistic state, and his assailants left him for dead. As you say, his wounds were fatal. His catatonic condition merely delayed the inevitable. Even this far from Buda-Pest, we are not cut off from news and gossip. I understand that Sandor's body was stolen from the morgue"—at this the Countess looked directly at Wellington, who felt suddenly uncomfortable—"and that, after much misadventure, the corpse vanished. Without being indiscreet, I can only tell you that his body was recovered by...friends. His remains have been cremated. It is unwise to involve yourselves any further in the affair."

"But there is still danger," Wellington protested. "His assailants may still be in the area. They must be found and turned over to the authorities."

"You place me in an awkward position." There was a twinkle of amusement in Bathory's eyes. "I can assure you that those responsible for the attack on Sandor are already dead. What court could ask for more?"

"Bram and I were more concerned with the council than the court."

Puzzled by the remark, Bathory frowned. "What do you mean?"

"Our remaining on at the university was dependent upon our providing Sandor's corpse for autopsy."

"You seem to be a very resourceful young man when it comes to overcoming obstacles. It's rare to find that sort of survival instinct in this day and age." Bathory regarded him with half-closed eyes. "You are studying to be a doctor, I believe?"

"Yes."

"Why? To aid those who suffer, or is it for the money and prestige?"

"Well, I...." Taken aback by her candor, Wellington's voice trailed off as he found himself at a loss for words.

Bathory smiled sympathetically at his embarrassment. "A little of all three, perhaps? There is no shame in reaping the rewards of a job well done."

"My motives aren't entirely mercenary," Wellington was quick to explain. "Bram and I both feel advances in medical science have the potential to prolong life."

"Prolonging life?" Bathory appeared impressed. She leaned across the table toward her guest, and Wellington felt himself drawn toward her. "I believe you and I may share a mutual interest." Barely had he heard her words when Wellington found Bathory suddenly standing next to him, leaning over him to speak softly in his ear. "Would you like to defeat death?" The question was more breath than whisper. The student turned to answer, only to find her mouth moving across his own. Her lips were soft and, as he closed her eyes to return the kiss, he felt an overwhelming desire to draw her down into the chair with him. Barely had the thought come to him when Bathory slipped onto his lap. As his arms encircled her shoulders, Wellington felt her warm moist mouth move to his neck. There was a sharp twinge of pain at his throat, and then his limbs grew weak and numb as darkness swallowed him.

8. Dark Angels.

"Will you play for me sometime?" Van Helsing asked Elga as they walked through the courtyard. It was the first time either of them had ventured outside since they had arrived at Bathory's estate. The wind was gone, and the late afternoon was warmed by the sun overhead. In spite of the improvement, he noticed Elga was still careful to cover her head with the hood of her cloak. Possibly it was to shade her eyes, as he noticed the sun reflecting off the snow seemed to cause her discomfort.

Elga smiled at his request. "If you'd like."

"One of your own compositions," Van Helsing admonished, "not some parroted piece taught to everyone whoever sat at a piano."

"Whatever you say, Bram." Elga gripped his elbow and guided him towards a large open archway near the rear of the estate. "But a private performance."

"Careful, or you'll have me feeling quite important."

In spite of the sun, Elga turned her face up to peer into his eyes. "Maybe you are."

"Surely you don't just write music and then never play it for anyone but yourself. Haven't you ever shared it?"

"I've played for my aunt, and for Carmilla." Still looking up at Van Helsing, her eyes squinting tight in the light, Elga managed a smile as she added, "And sometimes for special friends."

As they passed under the archway, a wooded glen lay before them. On the far side of it was a frozen pond. Dark patches dotted the snow, portions of a stone walkway leading down to the glade that peered out from beneath the sheet of white blanketing the ground. Van Helsing looked from the courtyard they had just left to the path that stretched out ahead. "How odd."

"What?" There was a touch of concern in Elga's voice. "Is something wrong?"

"The grounds, they don't seem to have nearly as much snow as we what waded through on the way here." Van Helsing started to step back into the courtyard. "Let's go across the moat to the main gate; I want to see what the roads look like."

"It's the way the castle and grounds were originally planned and built," Elga explained, taking his arm and leading him away from the manor. "The outer walls surrounding the main building act as a wind break, as do the woods around the rest of the property, creating a natural barrier against storms."

As the two made their way down the slippery slope, Van Helsing nearly lost his footing on the icy rock. "Here," Elga offered, slipping one arm around him for support, "I know the grounds better than you." Feeling foolish, the slight stinging sensation in Van Helsing's cheeks told him he was blushing and he hoped his companion would consider the winter weather responsible for the increased crimson in his face. He was sure the color deepened even more as Elga took one of his arms and guided it about her own waist and said, "Now just keep looking at me, and I'll guide you across the stones."

Van Helsing met Elga's gaze, and felt a sudden hush surround him. Unable to look away from her, unable to see anything but her, he was only vaguely aware that they were walking across the glen. Although she never looked ahead, Elga seemed to know exactly where she was going. Had he been able to take his eyes from his companion, Van Helsing might have found the sight of the snow parting before them, and then closing back after they had passed, somewhat unsettling. Suddenly they were in shade, as the path had wound into the woods.

"I seem to lose all sense of time and direction with you," Van Helsing said. Feeling disoriented, he glanced back over his shoulder at the pathway. What was wrong with the landscape? What was missing that should have been there?

"Come on, Bram, I want to show you something," Elga said. There was a touch of impatience and insistence in her voice. As she took hold of his wrist and lead him onward, Van Helsing realized he could not see any footprints in the snow along the trail they had just traveled. Turning to look ahead, he found the path through the woods growing clearer as the trees grew richer in color. Even the air was growing warmer. They soon came upon a small clearing where grass—green grass!—grew. A small chapel, long unused, stood at the far end of the clearing. The rocks of the ancient building, like those of the stone bench before it, were covered in rich, velvety green moss. Beyond the chapel lay an ancestral burial vault, the walls of which were cracked where sections of stone had long ago started to sink into the earth.

The gurgling of a nearby stream could be heard, and the soothing sound made Van Helsing feel as if he would slip into a deep sleep. A warm weight seemed to ease over his shoulders and his limbs began to grow heavy. While the world they had just left was in winter, here it was an autumn afternoon, cool but comfortable. He slowly removed his heavy cape and undid his shirt collar. Where was he? In a dream? "Yes," Elga's voice whispered in his ear, even though she was now nearing the chapel while he was still standing at the edge of the clearing. "It's all just a dream, my love."

Van Helsing was aware of moving towards Elga, but he could not tell if he was walking or gliding across the ground. Joining Elga he saw the stream that he had heard, which ran behind the chapel. There were ancient stone steps along the bank that led down to the water's edge, ending in a landing where boats once moored. Elga slipped her cloak off and guided him to the stream and the two of them sat together on the steps. Van Helsing started to gather up the edge of Elga's skirt to keep it from dipping down into the water, but she took his hand and kissed it, then slowly pressed him back against the smooth, worn stones.

Undoing Van Helsing's vest and shirt, Elga began to kiss his face and neck, caressing his chest and smiling as she felt his heart react to her touch. Warmth, followed by numbness, flowed through Van Helsing as Elga's soft mouth moved down along his jawline and onto his neck, where it hesitated before gently drifting across his shoulder. He noticed her breath had a peculiar, but not unpleasant odor, and suddenly found his eyelids growing heavy. Although he wanted to hug her, he could not seem to get his arms to move. A twinge of sadness passed through him at the thought of something lost. There was someone else, a name he had forgotten. What was it he had been worried about before coming to the castle?

With a sigh Van Helsing opened his eyes and found Elga's face was just inches from his, her eyes closing as her lips brushed against his own. Sensing a change in him she paused, her eyes searching deep into his as dim memories struggled to come back to him. Her mouth hovered over his and her words came out as breath rather than sound. "What is it, Bram?" She kissed the tip of his nose. "What is it you want to tell me?"

Van Helsing found it difficult to speak, as if the lethargy that held him had seized his speech. As he struggled to talk, his mind hazed over. "I...have...."

Elga's mouth curved into an enigmatic smile. "What? What do you have?"

"Someone…."

"Who, Bram? Who is it?"

"My fiancée."

Elga gently bit his right lobe. Her warm breath filled his ear as she whispered, "But you don't have a fiancée." Sitting up to see his face, she asked, "Will you forget about me, the way you forgot about her on the staircase last night? Do you even remember her name?"

Van Helsing fought to clear the mist from his mind. Was he dreaming or awake? He was with Elga and wanted it to be real, but there was the urge to leave, to get away from her and return to…where? Who? Maybe if he could look away from Elga he could sort out his thoughts. He could hear the running water as it rushed across the stones in the stream. Slowly, with a great deal of effort, he was able to turn his head toward the water. He wanted to plunge his hand into the cool clear current in hopes the sensation would revive his senses, but could not make his limbs move.

"Please stay here with me." Elga had taken his hand and placed it over her heart, pressing it close so that he could feel it. As her other hand slipped into his shirt, coming to rest over his own heart, he realized they were beating in rhythm. Once more her mouth moved to his and lingered just above it. "Stay with me," she repeated. She kissed him tenderly, gently forcing his mouth open with hers and slowly drawing the breath out of him. Again Van Helsing felt the urge to hold her closer, crush her body against his, but his muscles were paralyzed. Her mouth moved down to his neck, her lips caressing the flesh of his throat.

Looking down at Elga, Van Helsing tried to speak when something caught his eye. While he could see his own shadow beside them on the stone steps, behind Elga there was none. Barely had the thought registered with him when the distant chime of church bells tolling in the late afternoon air reached them. Elga shrieked, rearing up and clutching at her ears to shut out the sound.

As she opened her mouth to scream again it was Van Helsing's own voice that sounded, and he bolted upright to find himself on the ground in the snow-shrouded woods. In the dying light he saw a dark figure kneeling at his side, her cloak whipped about by the rising wind. Only when she spoke did he realize it was Elga.

"Bram, are you alright?" Even in the shadows he could see her face was filled with concern as she peered out at him from beneath her hood.

"What happened?" Van Helsing looked about, confused. Where was he, and how had he gotten there? Trying to focus, he heard the final notes of the bells fade away.

Elga seemed agitated, almost angry. "You slipped in the snow and hit your head against the trunk of this tree. I told you not to leave the path. I didn't think I would ever get you to wake up."

"I had the strangest dream."

"We have to go back," Elga insisted.

Even in the gathering gloom, Van Helsing recognized his surroundings. Pointing down the drifting path, he asked, "What's down there?"

"Nothing. Now come on; Aunt Elizabeth will be worried about us."

Van Helsing was not convinced. "There's a chapel there, isn't there? In a clearing by a stream."

"No, there's nothing down there. We mustn't stay here any longer; dinner will be waiting."

"There *is* a chapel, in a clearing by a stream," Van Helsing said. "I know it was more than just a dream." He tried to sit up and gather enough energy to stand, only to suddenly found himself in the vice-like grip of Elga's hand as she hauled him to his feet as if he were a doll.

"You're hurt," Elga said, releasing him. "We're going back. *Now.*"

When they reached the manor, Van Helsing and Elga found dinner—and Countess Bathory—waiting on them. Distressed over their absence, the Countess met them in the courtyard. Seeing she wore no cloak, Van Helsing started to apologize for causing her concern, but was waved into silence by his host.

"You should not be out after dark." Bathory shot a quick, reproachful glance at Elga, yet there was inquisitiveness behind the impatience. "After all, the grounds are unfamiliar to you, and to loose your way or your footing could be fatal under these conditions."

"I am to blame, Countess," Van Helsing interjected. "Otherwise, we would not have been away for so long. I seem to have had a mishap. Fortunately, your niece was there to watch over me."

Bathory took Van Helsing's head in both hands, studying him for signs of injury. Looking to Elga, she asked, "He seems little the worse for wear. Have you become his guardian angel?"

Avoiding Bathory's gaze, Elga blushed and said nothing.

Van Helsing smiled. "You must be right, Countess; how could anyone so pretty be anything but an angel?" The color in Elga's cheeks deepened. "Now if she only had wings...."

Elga's discomfort seemed to increase, and Bathory laughed in spite of herself, an almost harsh laugh. Like Elga earlier, the Countess was careful to cover her mouth as if to hide her mirth. Stepping forward to give the girl a comforting caress, Bathory looked at her niece as she spoke to Van Helsing, "She might surprise you. Even angels have to hide their wings to disguise their true nature when they want to move among men."

"Come, Countesses," Van Helsing offered each woman an arm. "Allow me to act as escort after having kept you both outside on such an evening. You'll catch your death...."

"Only our dinner is in danger of growing cold this night," Bathory reassured him. "Your friend Wellington awaits us inside, and I am sure that it is only a sense of honor over hunger that has kept him from starting without us."

Linking arms, with Van Helsing in the middle, the threesome marched into the manor.

*

After dinner, Bathory led her guests to a vaulted chamber that, in previous years, had been an opulent ballroom. An intricate cluster of cobwebs clung to the chandelier that hung like a crown over the center of the room. Already at work in the chamber were the carriage driver and the footman, as well as Ilona and a second maid, a dark-haired girl whom Van Helsing had heard addressed as Anouska.

"Yet another sad reminder of days long past," the Countess commented as the servants began to light candles throughout the ballroom to chase away the gloom. "Thanks to your presence, there is life here once more."

While Ilona busied herself at the fireplace, making sure it had enough wood, the coachman and footman struggled with the ropes of the chandelier, lowering it so that Anouska could light those candles as well. If Bathory had planned to use this room after dinner it was a wonder she had not already had it prepared, Van Helsing mused as he watched these last-minute preparations. As if in answer to his unspoken thought, the Countess apologized. "Unlike the old days, we no longer maintain a large retinue."

"It saves on revenue," Wellington observed.

"A large household is not easily moved; the fewer people one has to rely on, the better," was Bathory's simple reply.

"Your other niece, Lady Carmilla, is she feeling better?" Van Helsing asked. A fleeting look of annoyance crossed Elga's face.

"Carmilla is stronger today, thank you." Bathory seemed pleased at the concern. "Her old appetite has returned, and I hope she will be able to join us tomorrow evening for dinner." The chandelier fully lit and back into place, Countess Bathory motioned the servants away. "Leave us, now. All but you, Anouska; you will stay and play for us." Turning her attention back to her guests, Bathory explained, "A fortunate find; she has a skilled hand with the violin."

Anouska bowed to her mistress and then, in response to a quick movement of Bathory's eyes, went over to the great window that dominated the far end of the ballroom. Before the darkened panes stood a piano and, near it, a music stand, from which hung a violin and bow. Taking up the instrument and tucking it beneath her chin, the servant began to play. Melancholy music filled the room, slowly and gently at first, then becoming more lilting and lively as the musician picked up the pace.

Smiling her approval at Anouska, Bathory looked to see the effect of the music on her guests, commenting, "The gypsy blood never truly leaves us."

Although he was certain he had never heard the melody before, Van Helsing felt there was something vaguely familiar to the tune. He suddenly found himself keeping beat with the heel of one boot tapping against the floor and forced himself to sit still. The music struck a chord in Wellington as well, as he had begun to keep time with the one hand draped across the ankle of his crossed leg, anticipating the accelerating change in tempo.

"I think I know this," Wellington exclaimed. He quickly stepped across the room, seated himself at the piano and began to accompany Anouska. As if fueled further by this addition, Anouska began slowly swaying to her own tune. As her movements increased, so did the rhythm, and a wild undercurrent began to run through the melody. Like the pounding pulse of someone in terror, the tempo quickened until Anouska sliced at the strings with the bow. Wellington felt himself as much spectator as participant, as he found himself hypnotized by the fiddler's frenzied form and he could not recall his fingers playing with such speed.

"Yes!" Bathory applauded Anouska's abandon. "Let us have dancing once more!" The Countess swept across the room and caught Wellington by the hand, guiding him from the piano to glide across the floor to the music.

Elga looked at Van Helsing questioningly. Smiling, he stepped forward and, with a bow, said, "I fear my abilities as a dancer are somewhat limited, especially during periods of sobriety, but if you would do me the honor...?"

There was no need for an answer, as Elga's eyes glistened with joy at the request. She slipped her hands into his, and he was surprised at how cold they were as they joined the Countess and Wellington on the marble dance floor. Van Helsing noticed once more that when he was with Elga his surroundings seem blurred and he felt as if he were floating, carried by unseen arms. He longed to sink into her embrace, to curl up in her arms and go to sleep, never having to wake up and never having to leave her. Yet somewhere in the back of his mind was still a reluctance to let go of the past.

Elga clutched him as close to her as she could. "You're never near enough," she complained gently. Van Helsing started to reply, but Elga placed one hand over his mouth and whispered, "Don't say anything. I have so much I want to say to you and don't know how. There are some things I can't tell you...at least not yet. Do you like me, Bram? I don't mean as a friend, but...I want you to care about me."

"I...I don't know. If I could talk to Chris, to be sure...." The moment the words came out of his mouth Van Helsing regretted them. At the sound of Christine's name, he felt Elga stiffen and he knew she was hurt. She buried her face in his breast and they continued to dance in silence. He could feel the moist warmth of her tears and could feel her body gently tremble with silent sobs. Although no one else in the room seemed to take notice of either of them, he felt self-conscious for both himself and Elga and danced her over to a darkened corner. Feeling less on display, he softly kissed the top of her head and said, "It seems harder and harder to keep my hands off of you."

"Then don't try." Carefully wiping away her tears before looking up at him, Elga smiled hesitantly and then stood up on tiptoe to whisper in his ear, "I shall be so tender with you."

Van Helsing was confused by her words, and felt even guiltier for having made her cry. As he gently kissed the remaining tears from her eyes, Elga held him more tightly and he was amazed at the strength in her delicate-looking frame. Barely had the thought crossed his mind when he inadvertently pulled away from her, puzzled. Instead of the salty taste of tears he expected, there was the harsh coppery aftertaste that one found in blood. As Elga saw the crimson smear of her tears upon Van Helsing's lips, her eyes filled with fear.

“What's happened to your eyes?” Van Helsing asked, startled at how red they had become. “It's like all the blood vessels have burst in them.”

“It's nothing!” Elga's whisper was almost a hiss as she whirled away from him. “It's this room; after all the years of neglect, the dust in here irritates them.”

“Let me see,” Van Helsing insisted, taking her by the chin to turn her face toward him. Resisting at first, Elga reluctantly allowed him to examine her. “Perhaps some of those hours of medical studies will prove practical after all. There is an ointment that might relieve the irritation.”

Elga looked downward. "There's nothing you have that can cure this."

Van Helsing looked skeptical. "Of course, it could come from drinking too much," he teased. Her head whipped up to glare at him with a fleeting fierceness that he was unable to imagine could have ever existed within her. For a moment it was if both orbs blazed with an inner light, but he dismissed it as a trick of the flames reflected from the fireplace and the illusion faded as quickly as it had appeared.

"I'm tired," Elga said. "Please walk me to my room."

"I'm sorry if I upset you…." Van Helsing began.

"It's not that," Elga said, kissing him on one cheek. "The strain of having had to move, the excitement of this afternoon…it's all been too much too soon."

Van Helsing took Elga by the elbow and started to lead her across the ballroom. Only then did he realize that Countess Bathory and Wellington had already gone, yet Anouska continued to play. Elga and Anouska's eyes met. At a slight nod from Elga, the servant lowered her violin and gave a slight curtsey before leaving the room. Alone in the silence, the ballroom seemed suddenly larger than before.

"I can't imagine growing up in a house this size," Van Helsing said, glancing about the chamber. "I think I could get lost in just this one room."

"There's more room in the human heart than in all the houses of the world," Elga said softly, slipping her arm in his. "Yet it's still not large enough to hold all the happiness you make me feel."

Van Helsing turned to look at her and was about to reply when he noticed his reflection in the window near the piano. Frowning, he looked from the glass to the girl that stood between him and the window, and then back at the glass. There was no sign of Elga in the darkened pane. She followed his gaze and Van Helsing felt her tense up. Suddenly the window burst outward, shattered by an unseen force.

At the sound of breaking glass, Van Helsing sat upright in his chair. He found himself seated near the fireplace in the ballroom, a shattered wineglass at his feet. Looking up as a girl's giggle reached his ears, he found Elga standing over him.

"I'm surprised you held onto it as long as you did," Elga said, kneeling to pick up the pieces of the glass. "I was afraid to take it from you for fear of waking you. You looked so peaceful."

The clock on the mantle chimed the hour of midnight.

"How long have I been asleep?" Van Helsing asked, disoriented.

"Right after Anouska started playing. Aunt Elizabeth and Gerald spent the evening dancing, while *you* left me all alone."

"But we…we danced, didn't we?"

Elga shook her head. "Only in your dreams." She leaned over and kissed his forehead. "And in mine." She reached out and took his hands, pulling him to his feet. "It's time you were in bed."

Van Helsing allowed Elga to lead him out of the ballroom. He gave a final glance over one shoulder at the piano, only to find the heavy drapes drawn across the window behind it. Turning away, he did not notice the rustle of the cloth from the breeze outside passing through the broken panes behind it.

9. A Healthy Appetite.

It was nearly midday once more when Van Helsing awoke. Here, at Bathory's estate, time seemed to have little meaning. There were no classes to attend, no deadlines to meet, and seemingly few expectations from their hosts. The countess seemed content to spend most of her waking hours at night, with no real responsibilities requiring her to adhere to the more mundane schedule imposed upon the rest of the world. Even after waking, Van Helsing felt reluctant to leave his bed and lay for some time contemplating what to do.

Finally forcing himself to sit up, Van Helsing slowly got to his feet. The room seemed warm, almost too warm, even though the fire of last night had long since burned out in the hearth. Or maybe it was not so much that the room was hot, but that the air seemed heavy and ancient. Pulling back the drapes, he began to wrestle with the window and, after a brief struggle, managed to get it open, the diamond-shaped panes screeching at the strain. Apparently he was the first to use this room in many years. The crisp, cold draft of air that rewarded his efforts was not unpleasant.

Feeling his senses sharpened by the brisk breeze, he rubbed his face and neck, as if to massage the rejuvenating air into his muscles. At the touch of the rough stubble of his chin against his skin, Van Helsing decided the first order of business was to shave.

Within minutes water and soap had been turned into lather and, with the aid of a small shaving mirror from his saddlebag, he was soon gliding the straight razor carefully along the contours of his jawline. By now the oppressive atmosphere of the room had cleared, and a slight chill touched his spine as he finished.

Van Helsing pulled on his boots and gave himself a final check in the shaving glass, razor at the ready should it be needed. Passable enough, he thought at the sight of his reflection. After wiping his face down with a towel, he turned to pick up his vest from the back of a nearby chair and return the razor back to its leather pouch, only to find he was not alone. Halfway across the room, her back to the fireplace, the dark-haired girl stared silently at him, her eyes hungry and mocking. Startled at the sudden appearance of his visitor, he dropped the razor

"Elga!" Van Helsing managed a surprised smile. "I didn't hear you come in or notice you in the mir—" There was a hard glint in her eye at what he was about to say and his voice died in the middle of the word. There was something about her that was different. Was it the way she wore her hair? Yes, the hair flowed freely about her head and down her shoulders, but there was something else...something almost taunting about the manner of her mouth, and a cruelty to the eyes as they glistened in the shadows. Van Helsing took a step forward her as realization set in. "Carmilla?" More thought than speech, the question was barely a whisper spoken under his breath.

At the sound of her name the girl curtsied and smiled, but beneath the warmth there was something disturbing about her demeanor. "Abraham Van Helsing," she said with a slight nod of her head. "I have already heard so much about you."

Van Helsing suddenly felt self-conscious. "I've seen your portrait," he began, "but the painting that hangs in the main hall above the staircase doesn't begin to do you justice. You look even more like Elga than I would have thought possible."

“Given your affection for her, I should be flattered.” Carmilla’s mouth curved into a slight smirk. “Perhaps you find this form more appealing?”

For a moment Van Helsing would have sworn it was now his fiancée Christine who stood before the fireplace, but quickly dismissed it as a trick of light and shadow as Carmilla moved toward him. Passing through the shaft of sunlight streaming in through the window, she shuddered and started to swoon. Had Van Helsing not been close enough to catch her, Carmilla would have collapsed to the floor. He led her to the bed and, making sure she was securely seated, went to the windows.

"How inconsiderate of me," Van Helsing said, closing the glass and pulling the drapes shut. "Elga had told me you were sick, and here I have the windows open in the middle of winter." Suddenly aware of a throbbing pain in his thumb, he realized he must have sliced it when the razor slipped from his hand. "I seem to have cut myself," he managed an embarrassed smile. “I’m not going to make much of a surgeon if I can’t even handle a blade long enough to shave.” Glancing back at the razor on the floor, he absent-mindedly put the edge of his wounded thumb in his mouth.

Carmilla was beside Van Helsing before he even realized the girl had left the bed. "You must be careful." Her voice was low and soft. "You are no longer in the city. If the wound should become infected...." She took his injured hand in both of hers. "Here, let me." Her mouth touched the cut as if to kiss it, and a feeling of warmth and numbness filled Van Helsing. As her fingers gently caressed the back of his hand, she began to suck the blood from the wound. The intoxicating sensation that had suddenly gripped him grew deeper. Carmilla's breathing became slow and heavy, and Van Helsing found his own breath matching the rhythm of hers. Slowly she looked up at him, her eyes darker and deeper than before. "Has the pain gone yet?"

As Van Helsing tried to speak a paralysis seized him, as if the intensity of her gaze had sent him into a stupor. Carmilla's lips brushed lightly across his thumb to get a tiny drop of blood remaining. She ran her tongue down the inside of his thumb and kissed the center of his palm before playfully chewing at the fleshy area at the base of the thumb. Then, slowly but firmly, she bit deep into the skin and lapped up the pool of red that flowed from the puncture. Van Helsing felt as if he was falling and realized Carmilla was easing him back onto his bed.

Slipping onto the edge of the bed, never once pausing in her feast, Carmilla crouched protectively over Van Helsing, her posture like that of a predator guarding a carcass as it feeds upon it. Every so often a faint noise in the house would reach her ears and Carmilla's eyes would flash about, making sure there was no threat of interruption. She had to be careful not to take too much too soon. It would not do to gorge herself and end up looking like a bloated leech. The virgin blood of a man was a rare treat and, if she were very careful, she could make him last for several days. For the time being, she would drink slowly but steadily.

*

While the thin, red ribbon of blood had trickled down the vampire's throat, the day's shadows had grown longer. As the first bell chimed for supper that evening, Carmilla glanced quickly over her shoulder at the sound, her eyes blazing at the intrusion. Looking back down at Van Helsing's sleeping figure, wistful frustration replaced her annoyance. She touched his injured thumb, and blood streamed from the cut. Carmilla kissed the wound and the crimson flow stopped. With a regretful sigh she licked the remaining blood from his hand. "*Au revoir, chéri.*"

*

The second bell sounded for supper and Van Helsing awoke with a start, only to find himself alone in his room. Could it be evening already? He had spent the entire day in feverish, dream-filled sleep. But Carmilla…he was sure she had been real or, if their meeting was but a dream, it had been most vivid. He looked down at his hand, which ached. There were traces of a faint cut across his thumb and a painful bruise at its base. Remembering that he had received the cut when he dropped his razor, he went to pick up the blade. Dizziness swept over him as he stood, and he steadied himself against a bedpost. Van Helsing reached towards the night stand to pour himself a drink when he noticed that his razor was on the vanity with his toilet articles, all of which had been neatly placed back in order since their use earlier that day.

*

When Van Helsing went down to the dining room, everyone else had already been seated. At the head of the table sat Countess Bathory and on either side of her were her nieces, with Carmilla to her right and Elga to her left. Wellington was seated to the right of Carmilla, with an empty chair directly across from him allowing Van Helsing to take his place next to Elga. As he sat down Elga gave him a troubled look, in spite of his reassuring smile. Carmilla continued to look quietly at her plate, taking little notice of the new arrival.

Bathory spoke, obviously concerned at his absence, but glad to see he had finally joined them. "Forgive us for starting without you, but when you did not come down for breakfast or dinner...." The Countess let her voice trail off, waiting to see if the young man offered any explanation. When there was no response, she motioned for him to help himself, saying "I hope you like blood pudding. Our cook prides herself on it."

"I was worried about you, Bram." Elga spoke quickly and quietly as she clutched his injured hand.

Carmilla looked up, a hint of humor in her eyes. Van Helsing winced slightly at Elga's grasp, but it was enough for her to take notice. Turning his hand over, Elga saw the marks in his flesh. Sadness filled her face, as if he had done something to hurt her. Releasing him, she folded her hands in her lap and stared unseeing at the table before her. Elga's eyes suddenly locked onto Carmilla, and there was a look of hatred there that Van Helsing would have never thought possible in her.

"Do you feel well, Bram?" asked Countess Bathory. "You look...weary."

Carmilla daintily wiped at her mouth with her kerchief, and made a soft noise. A look of realization came over Bathory and she laughed at herself. “An increase in years causes a decrease in memory. I forget that you have not yet met my second niece, whose portrait I am told you have been admiring. May I present Lady Carmilla Karnstein. Carmilla, this is Abraham Van Helsing."

Van Helsing stood and kissed Carmilla's offered hand. He paused after doing so, realizing he held her hand in the one he had injured and again wondered if their earlier meeting had been just a dream. Carmilla followed his gaze and smiled.

Taking his seat once more, Van Helsing said, "Countess Karnstein, I would not have been so enchanted by your portrait had I seen the inspiration for it first. As magnificent as the work is, it barely reflects reality."

Pleased, Carmilla blushed slightly. "I feel as if we have already met; Elga has spoken at great length about you. She's been quite good to keep me company during my illness."

"I trust that you are feeling better?"

"Much better, thank you." Carmilla smiled warmly. "I should be fully recovered very soon."

Van Helsing noticed a tear on Elga's cheek, and was surprised at how dark it appeared in the candlelight.

"More wine," Bathory commanded as Anouska came into the room and poured what was left in the crystal decanter into Van Helsing’s glass. "Something special for our guests."

The smell of the food, coupled with not having ate since the previous evening, made Van Helsing acutely aware of how hungry he was. He had not even swallowed the mouthful of meat when he drained his wineglass, downing food and drink together.

"I like to see a young man with a healthy appetite," Bathory said, pleased at Van Helsing's zeal at the meal.

"Almost unhealthy," Wellington added. "Slow down a bit, Bram, or you're going to make yourself sick. Don't wolf it down; take time to chew."

"Looks like you could do with another helping or two," Van Helsing said, noticing for the first time his friend's pallor. "You're as white as a sheet."

Wellington smiled good-naturedly at the rebuff. "Probably more from lack of sleep than lack of nourishment."

"I fear I'm to blame for your friend's condition." Bathory's tone was apologetic. "The nights are long and lonely for a stranger who has yet to become acquainted with the area and its people, and I have been imposing myself upon Master Wellington. No doubt my attentions have taxed him."

"We'll have to make sure he gets plenty of red wine and red meat," Van Helsing said. "It's good for the blood."

Carmilla began to giggle and covered her mouth. The sudden shift in Elga's posture made Van Helsing sure she had just kicked her cousin under the table. Although she grew quiet, there was still laughter in Carmilla's eyes as she met Elga's reproachful gaze.

"I didn't mean to doubt your diagnosis, Herr Van Helsing," Carmilla said. "Elga tells me you are a medical student."

"Former medical student," Van Helsing corrected. "At the moment, I don't seem to be serving any particular purpose."

"You shouldn't worry about the past." Carmilla leaned forward, reaching across the table to place a reassuring hand over his. "I'm sure, one day soon, you are going to prove very useful."

Elga stood, dropping her napkin onto her plate. "Please excuse me; I don't have much of an appetite."

"More for me," Carmilla said under her breath as she watched her cousin leave.

10. Predators and Prey.

There was still no sign of Elga after dinner. As Bathory and Wellington went into the library to play chess, leaving Carmilla and Van Helsing alone at the dining table, the medical student suddenly found himself feeling awkward. He disliked the challenge of trying to make small talk with a stranger. Since Carmilla had brought up his medical studies earlier, perhaps he would not seem too bold if he were to inquire about the nature of her illness. If he could encourage her to talk about herself, he might discover some mutual interest that would allow for a real conversation rather than simply a polite exchange of pleasantries.

"You mentioned Elga spending so much time with you while you were sick. I hope it was nothing serious…?"

"I have a rare form of anemia," Carmilla said, smiling at his concern.

"You know, doctors have been working to perfect the process of transfusing blood from one being to another."

Carmilla shuddered. "I thought the practice had been banned after the deaths of so many patients."

"You're talking about early experiments from nearly 200 years ago," Van Helsing said with a laugh. "This is the 19th century; they no longer infuse the blood of animals into that of humans. We work with a far more enlightened science, carefully matching the blood of men with men and women with women."

Swaying slightly in her chair, Carmilla raised one hand to her forehead as her other hand went to the table to steady herself. Van Helsing was immediately on his feet to catch her should she faint, but she waved him away. "It's nothing," she said. "All this talk of blood...."

"Forgive me," Van Helsing apologized. "I've been rather insensitive. Christine is so accustomed to such discussions that I forget how inappropriate many find these topics to be."

"Christine?" Carmilla asked.

"I was engaged."

"You must tell me more about her one day." Carmilla rose. "Please, if you will excuse me?" She took a step away from her chair, only to grip the edge of the table firmly to remain upright.

Fearing she was about to collapse, Van Helsing vaulted across the table and took Carmilla by the shoulders. "You must let me walk you to your room," he insisted.

Carmilla started to protest until seeing the resolve in his eyes. Growing solemn, she looked down "You shall think me a useless nuisance."

"You've been ill," Van Helsing said, "and taking care of the sick is what I've been trained to do."

As Van Helsing began to lead her from the dining room, Carmilla smiled demurely. Her voice was soft and hesitant as she asked, "Does this make me your first patient?"

"You have that dubious distinction." Van Helsing returned her smile. "And my first official prescription is less talking and more walking…at least until we get you safely upstairs."

As the two ascended the great staircase in silence, their footsteps echoing in the great hall, Carmilla gripped Van Helsing's arm tightly for support. As with Elga, he found the girl's grasp to be surprisingly strong, especially considering her affliction. Reaching the landing, Van Helsing paused before the portrait of Carmilla. Looking from the painting to her, he frowned.

"What is it?" Carmilla asked.

"I just now noticed the approach the artist used when painting you. That was a style very popular in the late 17th century."

At this, Carmilla firmly but gently guided Van Helsing up the steps and away from the painting. "Anatomy and art…two very diverse subjects. And I am told you handle the scalpel and saber with equal skill. You are proving to be quite the Renaissance man, Herr Van Helsing."

"Call me Bram."

Upon reaching the door to Carmilla's room, Van Helsing started to wish her goodnight. Before he could speak Carmilla looked up at him with a slightly pleading expression, her dark eyes almost black in the shadows of the corridor. "Please, will you come inside for a moment? Climbing the steps has made me feel lightheaded. If you would just make sure I get to my bed…?"

Feeling the warm prickling sensation that filled his face, Van Helsing hoped his embarrassment at the request did not show in the dark hallway. If he were going to become a doctor, he would have to get used to such circumstances. "Of course," he said as Carmilla opened the door. "I wouldn't want my reputation ruined outside your bedroom." Carmilla raised a questioning eyebrow at the comment as the corner of her mouth curled into a slight smile, a smile that grew as Van Helsing tried to quickly correct himself. "I mean, with you being my first patient, I have to make sure nothing happens to you—"

Carmilla gently placed one hand over his mouth before he could say any more. "I don't think you'll have to worry about your reputation," she said, slipping into the room. "If anyone can restore me, you can...*Doctor* Van Helsing."

"Not doctor yet," Van Helsing replied, following her inside but careful to keep the door open. Noticing the dying flame in the fireplace, he grabbed another log from the wood box and tossed it onto the grate. Taking the nearby poker, he knelt down and began to stir up the embers. "Your hands are as cold as ice. Let me get a proper fire going in the hearth."

Within minutes a healthy blaze burned cheerfully before him. Returning the poker to its holder, Van Helsing started to stand when he heard the door to the hallway close. Startled, he looked toward the door but saw no one there. Faint laughter reached his ears, but did not seem to come from any particular direction. Turning, he saw Carmilla standing near the bed, eyes glistening in the firelight. Her hair flowed down her shoulders and across a pale silken nightgown that seemed woven out of mist. Behind her, the curtains had been drawn back to allow the milky moonlight pour into the room.

Before Van Helsing could speak he felt his skin tingle, a sensation he had once felt when a lightning storm had left the air charged with electricity. The popping and crackling of the fireplace behind him could no longer be heard, leaving a sudden silence. The dancing shadows of the flickering flames grew dim and the room itself faded into a haze. There was only Carmilla, her body bathed in moonlight. Van Helsing was not sure if he had come to her or if she had come to him, but Carmilla now stood directly before him. Slowly she eased him to his knees and knelt beside him. She began to undo his cravat and then opened his shirt before clutching him to her to warm herself against his flesh. Tightening her embrace, she pressed his head against her breast and softly stroked his hair.

"Dear Bram, I believe Elga is truly in love with you," Carmilla's voice was soft and soothing. "Yet she holds back, hoping that the impossible will become possible, that you could love her and still remain just as you are. Perhaps she fears you are fragile and might break, like a delicate china doll. She is afraid to harm you, but the pain is fleeting and the outcome…everlasting." Carmilla put her lips to Van Helsing's ear and whispered, "But Elga will not have you."

Carmilla rose, lifting Van Helsing with her. Suddenly he found himself on her bed, Carmilla's face just above his own as she peered into his eyes and he felt as if she were searching his soul. Van Helsing tried to look away, hoping to focus on something—*anything*—so that she could see no more, but the fixtures and furniture of the room were indistinct silhouettes. Carmilla kissed him and rested her head upon his shoulder.

Taking his left hand into her right, Carmilla raised it up to examine his palm. She ran one finger across the spot where she had bitten him. "This is my mark that you bear. I am the one who drank from you and I shall be the one to take you."

Van Helsing's mind and senses were awake but his body seemingly slept, as he found himself unable to move. As Carmilla looked at him intently he could hear her thoughts, like a faint voice drifting across a great distance. "You belong to me…and only me." His heart beat rapidly against his ribs, as if it were about to burst. Carmilla softly ran her hand along his face, then down his neck and across his chest before it came to rest palm-down upon his stomach. She bent closer to him, her nostrils flaring like those of a wolf at his scent. Kissing him lightly on the lips and neck, her mouth moved down to hover directly over his convulsing heart. She began to kiss the feverish flesh of his chest, slowly at first and then more passionately, her teeth nipping at the skin. The more frenzied her affections the slower Van Helsing's heart became, as if Carmilla were taking the life from him. Her heartbeat increased as his decreased, a dull throb swelling through him with each labored beat.

Leaning up to look at Van Helsing's listless features, Carmilla's mouth opened to reveal the lustrous white teeth, the canines longer and sharper than the rest. Van Helsing trembled as he felt her warm moist breath on his neck before her mouth moved from his throat to his cheek to kiss him, and her long dark hair poured down around his head. His lips parted to receive hers and, as they kissed, through half-closed eyes Van Helsing was surprised to see an unexpected softness in her expression, the hunger replaced with a look of yearning. But the hunger of the hunter returned and he found Carmilla's mouth suddenly devouring his with wild passion. Van Helsing felt he must have passed out, for he could no longer see Carmilla and a sense of calm and well-being came over him, as if he were adrift upon a placid lake. There was a sharp stinging sensation at this throat, immediately followed by a rush of warmth.

Van Helsing lost all sense of time, unsure if it had been minutes or hours before he was aware of Carmilla's presence again, her bloodstained lips brushing against his. "I must replace what I've taken from you," she whispered. She bit into her lower lip until blood streamed from it, and then pressed her mouth firmly against his to kiss him with even more passion than before. A warm, salty taste began to fill Van Helsing's mouth and he tried to break free of her embrace. Her hand went to his throat and gripped it tightly, her thumb pressing against his Adam's apple, forcing him to swallow her blood as she continued the kiss. Suddenly Van Helsing felt a change come over him; his heart seemed to surge and his mind raced as Carmilla's thoughts burst into his brain, flooding his mind with endless images and experiences encountered across the ages.

Van Helsing felt the use of his limbs come back to him. Taking Carmilla in his arms, he pulled her tighter to him. Again her mouth moved to his neck, her tongue lapping at the blood that still trickled from the puncture wounds she had made there earlier. As her fangs penetrated his flesh again to reopen the wounds and allow the blood to flow more freely, a sharp wrenching pain tore through Van Helsing as Carmilla was ripped away from him by Elga and tossed across the room like a rag doll.

Elga's voice was a snarl as she confronted Carmilla. "How could you?" The words were more accusation than question. Her gaze blazed red, which Van Helsing dismissed as an illusion of her eyes reflecting the flames of the fireplace. "How could you?" she repeated, her voice now a tear-filled whisper.

Recovering, Carmilla shrugged. "*Carpe nocturna*." She was unable to suppress a smile at the animal fury burning in Elga's eyes at the remark, but then frowned as a distant sound reached her ears.

Keeping a wary eye on Elga, who seemed like a cat waiting to pounce upon its prey, Carmilla made her way to the window. Opening it, she noticed the dark clouds on the horizon silhouetted against the lead-grey sky. It would be morning soon. Again came the strange sounds and this time she was just able to detect faint voices, one of which seemed familiar. Carmilla turned to look back at Elga. "Why don't I leave the two of you alone? I'm sure you would like some privacy to say your farewells."

Before Elga could reply Carmilla had slipped through the window, her body plummeting toward the ground. Her skin darkened and her ears and nose extended. Talons grew from her fingers as her outstretched arms became the wings of an enormous bat, a demonic creature that caught the currents of air and swooped upward toward the turret that towered over the courtyard.

At the massive iron gates of Bathory's estate, Lieutenant Markus and Major Arcana attempted to pry the lock apart with their swords. From his saddle General Spielsdorf looked toward the ancient stone structure that awaited them on the other side of the moat. Even in the early morning gloom he could see parts of the structure had crumbled away over the centuries, but it still remained a forbidding fortress. There was the sharp snap of steel, followed by a stream of profanity from Markus as he held up the broken blade of his saber.

Arcana drew his pistol. "Perhaps a lead ball through the lock will be as good a key as any."

Spielsdorf made no attempt to hide his contempt at the suggestion. "Why not simply send up a flare into the air and announce our arrival?"

"It's neither lock nor rust that binds those gates," said Father Florescu, the priest who accompanied the small party on their mission to destroy the undead. Holding the reins of his own horse as well as those of Markus and Arcana in his left hand, he crossed himself with his right and then spoke again. "They've been sealed by Satan. You should have brought the rest of your regiment; they could have broken through—"

"And aroused the whole house," Spielsdorf said, cutting him off. "The fewer men, the less chance of attracting attention."

Dr. Paole, the fifth and final member of the group, swung down from his horse and started to unbuckle one of his saddle bags. "I may have some acid here. Not much, but perhaps enough to weaken the hinges."

Spielsdorf produced a tiny vial from the folds of his cloak. "I've something stronger than acid." Ignoring the inquiring looks of his companions, the general hurled the bottle at the gate. The fragile cylinder shattered into a shower of glass slivers against the lock, and the liquid it contained steamed as it streamed down the blackened iron. The gates shuddered and swung inward, the groans of metal grinding against metal greeting them.

"Holy water, Father," Spielsdorf explained as Markus and Arcana took to their saddles. "Let's make our way quickly and quietly across the bridge. As long as it has taken us to find Bathory's estate, I hope we're not too late."

In Carmilla's room Van Helsing sat on the edge of the bed, his senses restored to him now that Carmilla had gone. "I'm sorry, Elga," he whispered hoarsely as he stared at the floor, unable to meet her gaze. "I never meant to hurt you."

Even though he could not see it, Elga gave him a sympathetic smile. She sat down beside him and took his hands in hers. "It wasn't your fault, Bram. You didn't know what you were doing."

"But I did," Van Helsing insisted, finally looking up at her. "I knew exactly what I was doing. I wanted her. I don't know why, but I—"

Elga placed one hand over his mouth to keep him from saying more. "You wanted her because *she* wanted you to want her." Seeing the unspoken question in his eyes, she felt it was time to tell him what she had wanted but feared to for so long. "We're...." For the first time since they had met, Elga made no attempt to hide her face as crimson tears streamed from her eyes, glistening like liquid rubies in the dying firelight. "We're vampires, Bram." Her voice was so soft that Van Helsing was barely able to make out her words.

"What?"

"Carmilla, Aunt Elizabeth...even me."

"You're joking, of course." Van Helsing started to laugh but stopped as he studied her face, realizing she actually believed what she had just told him.

"No, dearest. Remember Sandor, the man whose body you and Gerald stole from the morgue?"

Van Helsing was stunned. "How could you possibly know about that?"

Reaching up, Elga slowly caressed his cheek. "I was there that night. Sandor was one of us; that's why he attacked you. Aunt Elizabeth changed him."

"But it's not possible." Van Helsing shook his head in disbelief. "It's like something out of the Brothers Grimm."

"Grim enough," Elga replied, a hint of irony in her eyes. "Sandor was dead when you first found him…but he didn't stay that way, did he?" She took one of his hands and placed it over the puncture wounds on his throat. "You have Carmilla to thank for that. It would have been different with me; I would have never forced myself on you or forced you to do anything against your will."

"But Carmilla is gone," Van Helsing said.

Elga tried to keep her voice calm, fighting back the bitterness she felt. "You belong to her now. She didn't just drink your blood, she gave you her own." Taking his head in her hands, she whispered, "Come closer." As Van Helsing leaned forward she gently kissed the bruises Carmilla had left around his mouth and neck. There was a tingling sensation at the touch of her lips, and the bruises began to fade. "That's all I can do for you. Keep your collar buttoned and it will hide the punctures." She gave him a final, lingering kiss.

As Elga stood, the sound of hooves on stone drifted in through the open window where Carmilla had vanished. Going to the window, Elga saw General Spielsdorf and his men entering the courtyard. Maybe it would be better this way. Turning back to Van Helsing, she gave him a bittersweet smile and said, "This may be the last time we ever see each other. Remember me."

"Of course I'll remember you," Van Helsing said. "But where are you going?"

"I want you to remember *everything*."

"I don't understand."

Elga's voice was a soft, hollow whisper. "You will, when the time comes."

Van Helsing suddenly realized he could see the dim morning light from the window behind Elga, seeping through her as if she were a phantom. Her features grew indistinct, a transparent figure of fog rather than flesh and blood. Before he could overcome his shock and make an effort to stop her, Elga's spectral form had dissolved into tendrils of mist that trickled out the window. The window slammed shut, as if by an unseen hand, and resisted Van Helsing's efforts to force it open.

In the library, Wellington looked wearily at the marble and onyx chessboard on the small round table before him. The ancient Chinese playing pieces, also carved from marble and onyx, appeared to be silently gloating at his impending defeat. With a sigh he made what he knew would be his final move.

"Checkmate," Countess Bathory said, moving her queen into position.

"I've lost count of how many times history has repeated itself this evening," Wellington said, shifting in his chair in hopes of reviving his circulation if not his spirits. "You are not an easy conquest."

"That depends upon your approach," Bathory replied. She noticed the clock on the mantelpiece. "Oh dear, it's very nearly morning. I've wasted away your entire night."

"A night with you could hardly be considered wasted," Wellington reassured her.

Blushing, Bathory stood and picked up the nearly empty brandy decanter and the two matching crystal glasses resting beside the chessboard. "You should be careful with your words; some might mistake gallantry for carnality."

As Bathory took the set of crystal over to the long wooden table that filled the center of the room, Wellington felt his own face grow flush and attempted to quickly clear up any confusion. "I merely meant—"

"I'm flattered, either way," Bathory said, cutting him off as she glanced back at Wellington over one shoulder. Returning to him, she slowly slipped her hands into his clothes to tear away the cloth and expose his throat and chest. As their eyes met, Wellington's gaze glazed over. Bathory's mouth clamped over the puncture wounds beneath his jawline and bit into them until she could feel the red river of life gush out and rush into her once more. She smiled to herself as she felt his hands begin to explore her body.

Finally Bathory finished her feast and looked up at Wellington, only to find herself feeling almost wistful. He would only last another night, and she realized she might actually miss him. Wellington tilted his head down and kissed her, his lips feverish against her cool skin. The act was gentle at first, but increased in passion as it was repeated until fierceness replaced affection in both of them. Pulling away from him with a laugh, Bathory's fingertips touched her bloodstained lips and she grew thoughtful.

"Stay with me." Bathory's voice was hesitant, and Wellington was not sure if her words were intended as a command or a request. Slipping her gown down from her shoulders, the countess ran her thumb beneath one breast, her nail silently slicing into the skin until a scarlet stream began to trickle from the opening in her flesh. "This is my blood, the most precious thing I have. Drink from me, and you need never know death."

A sudden shower of blood splattered across Wellington's face as the tip of an arrow burst through the flesh between Bathory's breasts. Whirling, she saw Lieutenant Markus standing in the doorway of the library, a crossbow in his hands. Animal fury replaced the disbelief in her eyes, her teeth gnashing as she clawed at the arrow to pull the wooden shaft from her heart. Her desperation grew as she saw her hands became gnarled with age.

"Yes, Countess," Markus said, cautiously entering the room, "the years are starting to catch up with you." Tossing the crossbow onto the table, where it crashed into the crystal decanter Bathory had just placed there, Markus pulled the two great Kukri knives from their sheaths on the back of his heavy leather belt.

Bathory, still struggling to remove the arrow, turned to Wellington and pleaded, "Help me!" The young man could only watch in shock as Bathory's hair began to turn from gold to silver, unable to understand what was happening before his horrified eyes. Suddenly the arrow started to yield and the countess had pulled it halfway out of her bosom when Markus severed her hand from the wrist with one Kukri blade before bringing the second knife slicing through the air to decapitate her. As her head spun past Wellington to strike the chessboard, scattering the playing pieces across the floor, the medical student fought the urge to become violently ill. The body and head aged centuries within seconds and were quickly reduced to dust.

Markus sat the Kukri knives on the table next to the crossbow and bent to examine the wounds on Wellington's neck. With Bathory dead, the punctures were already closing over and healing. Giving Wellington a reassuring smile, he asked, "Are you all right?"

Before Wellington could answer, Carmilla's voice came from behind Markus. "*The Bible* claims sins must be cleansed by blood." The soldier turned to see Carmilla standing between him and the long table, her arms crossed with one of his Kukri knives in each hand. "You have sinned, have you not?" She lashed out, the blades blurring as she brought them together in an almost scissor-like fashion to slice his head from his shoulders. Barely had his body hit the floor than Carmilla was beside it, lapping up the rapidly pooling blood like an animal dying of thirst. She looked up, her dark orbs burning deep into Wellington's soul as they made eye contact. Wellington trembled at the hunger he saw in her stare.

“Up here,” General Spielsdorf’s voice called out from the upper floor. There was the sound of rushing boots on the stone steps in answer to the summons and, with an unholy hiss, Carmilla’s lips pulled away from her teeth in frustrated rage. The expression reminded Wellington of a cat about to attack.

“Be patient, *mon ami,*” Carmilla said. “There will be other opportunities for me to finish what Aunt Elizabeth began.” Half turning/half twisting away from Wellington, Carmilla sprang toward the door and landed on all fours as she fled, the act accompanied by the padding of paws on the floor as female became feline. In the guise of a cat, Carmilla slipped past Father Florescu without attracting attention as he came into the library.

Van Helsing was still standing at the open window in Carmilla’s room, hoping to spot some trace of Elga, when General Spielsdorf and Dr. Paole found him. The medical student remained unaware of their arrival until Spielsdorf asked, “You are Abraham Van Helsing?”

“Vampires,” was all Van Helsing said, slowly turning away from the window to look at the newcomers. “She said they were vampires.”

Spielsdorf nodded sympathetically. “Yes, there are such things.”

“But it’s not possible,” Van Helsing said, shaking his head. “I’ve seen them out during the day…all three of them.”

“Which makes them even more dangerous. Only those who are very old and very powerful are able to do that, although the daylight weakens them.” The general gestured for Dr. Paole to examine Van Helsing. The doctor led the young man to a chair and studied the wounds on his throat as Spielsdorf continued to talk, “Most vampires do not survive very long, usually dying through ignorance or arrogance. Upon becoming one of the undead, they don't learn to separate fact from fiction about their condition. Others become overconfident, confusing immortality with invulnerability. They believe that, because they cannot grow old or die from natural causes, they cannot be killed. As a result, they fail to take the necessary precautions or start to take unnecessary risks. This can be especially true if they become obsessed with someone. They are so focused on desire and gratification that they let their guard down."

"How many of them fed on you?" Paole asked as he completed his examination.

"Just one…the one called Carmilla."

Coming closer to look at Van Helsing's bloodstained lips, Spielsdorf grew grim and asked, "Did you drink from any of them?" Getting no immediate response, the general grabbed Van Helsing by the front of his shirt and yanked him to his feet as he impatiently repeated the question. "Answer me, boy; did you drink from any of them?"

"Yes." Van Helsing's response was almost inaudible. "From Carmilla."

Spotting one of the doors to the stable standing ajar, Major Arcana dashed across the courtyard on foot, his saber drawn. He had almost reached the twin doors when they burst open as a horse and hearse raced out, nearly crushing the soldier between hoof and wheel. Arcana threw himself to one side, landing face down on the frozen ground as the speeding vehicle splattered him with snow and ice, unaware that his saber had been snapped in half beneath its wheels. Recovering, he leaned up on one elbow to see no driver sat in the seat of the hearse. A white coffin with gold handles and inlay bounced about in the back as the conveyance raced toward the bridge to cross the moat.

Getting to his feet, Arcana cursed at the discovery of his broken blade but kept a tight grip on what remained of the saber. Realizing there would be no chance of overtaking the hearse, he cautiously entered the stable. The sight of the five bodies piled near one of the stalls chilled him more than the arctic air outside. Using the jagged tip of his saber, Aranca turned the top body over to find Ilona's lifeless eyes staring up at him. Beneath her lay the body of Anouska, and the soldier saw the savage wounds on their throats. No doubt the remaining three were the corpses of the cook, footman and coachman.

As the sound of voices outside reached his ears, Arcana went to the door. General Spiesldorf, Dr. Paole and Father Florescu were coming out of the manor, accompanied by Van Helsing and Wellington. "Where's Markus?" Arcana called out.

"Dead," Spielsdorf said. "Along with Bathory. That still leaves us with two."

"One," Arcana corrected. "A coffin just left here, and it's a safe bet it was not empty. The servants are in here, dead."

"Are you sure?" Spielsdorf asked.

"Whoever escaped made quick work of the staff; I don't think there was time for anything more."

Spielsdorf peered into the stables at Aranca's discovery. "That looks like Carmilla's handiwork. By gorging herself, she could go into hiding and survive in a deep sleep for some time before needing to feed again. We'll burn the bodies, just to be sure."

"I don't understand," Van Helsing said, exchanging a glance with Wellington.

"Not every victim of a vampire becomes a vampire," Spielsdorf said. "If they did, the world would have been overrun with the undead centuries ago. It's not enough to have been bitten by one of these foul things; you must also drink their blood."

Arcana nodded. “Such occurrences are rare, as they prefer to keep their numbers few and competition to a minimum. These are very territorial creatures.”

Spielsdorf’s eyes narrowed as he bit his lip in thought. “Bathory is dead and Carmilla has fled….” The general slowly looked about the courtyard, as if silently searching for something, before finally asking “So where is Elga?” Van Helsing felt uneasy at hearing Spielsdorf mention her name. The general seemed to sense his discomfort and turned, looking him sharply in the eye as he asked, “Is there a crypt on the grounds, or a family vault beneath the estate?”

“Countess Bathory never mentioned a burial vault….” Van Helsing’s voice trailed off as Elga’s words came back to him: *I want you to remember everything.*

“What is it, Bram?” Wellington asked.

“There’s a chapel,” Van Helsing said, frowning as he tried to remember what seemed a distant dream, “a chapel somewhere in the woods, with an ancestral crypt behind it. Elga took me there.”

Spielsdorf’s eyes glistened with anticipation. “Can you find it again?”

“Through there,” Van Helsing said, pointing to an archway at the far end of the courtyard. “There’s a pathway through there that leads to it.”

“Gather our things,” Spielsdorf instructed Arcana. “If we find what I think we will, it’s going to be wet work.” Turning to Dr. Paole and Father Florescu, he nodded to the stables. “Take those bodies and whatever you can find inside, hay or wood, and build a fire.”

“Fire or pyre?” Paole asked.

"Show some pity…and piety," Florescu said, unamused by the jest. "How do you know we won't share their fate before this is all over?"

*

With Van Helsing in the lead, the party of four rode single file through the trees toward the chapel. General Spielsdorf was directly behind him, followed by Wellington as Major Arcana brought up the rear. As they came into the clearing, Van Helsing felt disoriented. While he was sure he had really been here before, the reality did not match his memory. The stone chapel had slowly sunk into the ground over the years, causing it to now lean at an odd angle. Behind it was the mausoleum, the roof of which was in partial ruin.

Bringing their horses to a halt, they dismounted. Spielsdorf reached into his pocket and brought out two silver chains, each of which had a tiny crucifix attached to the end, and handed them to Van Helsing and Wellington. "This will protect you from her, and others of her kind."

"I don't need protection from her," Van Helsing said, reluctant to take the gift. "Elga tried to protect *me*. I have nothing to fear from her; she loves me."

"Bram, listen to me," Spielsdorf said, pressing the crucifix into his hand. "Vampirism isn't seduction, it's rape; rape of the soul."

As the general and Major Arcana set to work with hammer and chisel on the door of the tomb, Wellington held his crucifix up and scrutinized it skeptically. "Well, I suppose it would make Mum and Dad happy."

Van Helsing was amazed at his friend's words. "After all we've been through, and yet you still don't believe?"

"I've *seen* vampires," Wellington said, pocketing the cross. "But I've still not seen God."

The creaking of ancient rusted hinges announced the soldiers' success at forcing open the doorway to the tomb. Spielsdorf entered first. Small snowdrifts had formed across the floor, and a shaft of cold morning light poured into the mausoleum through a hole in the roof to spill upon a marble sarcophagus in the middle of the chamber. For a fleeting instant Spielsdorf thought a young girl was asleep on the massive lid, and then realized it was a life-size carving of the coffin's occupant, the contrasting combination of light and shadow on the sculpture making the marble figure even more life-like. Cut deep into the side of the stone coffin was a cryptic inscription.

COUNTESS DOLINGEN OF GRATZ
SOUGHT, AND FOUND, DEATH IN STYRIA
1701

Spielsdorf was suddenly aware he was no longer alone in the tomb and turned to find Arcana next to him. Behind them, standing inside the doorway, were Van Helsing and Wellington. Van Helsing stared at the marble figure of Elga, his eyes glistening in the gloom of the room.

"Help me with the lid," Spielsdorf said.

The two soldiers struggled to move the massive slab aside. At length they had slid it to an angle to reveal Elga at rest inside, her unseeing eyes staring up at the ceiling. Spielsdorf glanced over at Van Helsing, who slowly approached the coffin. Standing at the edge, he peered down at her face as a single tear of blood trickled down her cheek.

"She knows," Van Helsing whispered, taking a step back.

"Yes," Spielsdorf said, placing a comforting hand upon Van Helsing's shoulder. "Even in this catatonic state, she is aware of all that goes on around her." Spielsdorf looked over at Wellington and, with a slight movement of his head, signaled for him to take his friend away.

As Wellington took Van Helsing by the elbow and started to guide him toward the door, Van Helsing saw Arcana remove a mallet and something else from a black leather satchel he had been carrying. He hesitated, but Wellington's grip became firm and he once again allowed himself to be led away. Suddenly he stopped at the doorway and turned to see General Spielsdorf drive the wooden stake into Elga's heart. A geyser of blood erupted from her chest and Elga screamed, crimson foam spewing from her mouth. Van Helsing felt his legs give out beneath him. He could no longer see the hellish scene; there was only darkness as his head struck the cold marble floor.

11. Through Other Eyes.

When Van Helsing regained consciousness, he found Carmilla staring down at him with dark soulless eyes. He bolted upright with a cry, only to realize he was gazing at the portrait of her that had hung in the great hall of Countess Bathory's estate and which now rested on a chair near his bed. Dizzy and disoriented, he looked about but did not recognize the room. The painting was the only familiar furnishing to be found in his strange surroundings. At the sound of a key in the lock, Van Helsing tensed up until the door opened to reveal Wellington standing there, a look of relief on his face at seeing his friend was finally awake.

"What is this place?" Van Helsing asked.

"We're back in Buda-Pest," Wellington said. "This is one of General Spielsdorf's rooms. Apparently he and his entourage have engaged this entire floor of the hotel for their activities."

"Buda-Pest?" Van Helsing rubbed the back of his neck.

"You've been out for several days, and had quite a fever." Wellington sat on the edge of the bed. "Dr. Paole was afraid you were going to slip into a coma. How are you feeling?"

“A little light-headed.” Van Helsing gave a slight nod toward the painting. “And then waking up to *that*….”

Wellington’s mouth turned down into a frown. “My fault, I’m afraid. We’ve been taking turns keeping watch over you, and I brought that in here to study it last night.” Van Helsing’s hand went to the puncture wounds on his throat. “They’re still there,” Wellington said in response to the gesture and then quickly changed the subject. “Why don’t I send down for some breakfast?”

“Elga…?” Van Helsing whispered the word.

“She’s dead now, Bram; *really* dead.” Wellington paused for a moment, and then smiled. “You know, when we got back into town, I very nearly joined her.”

Puzzled, Van Helsing looked at him questioningly and then suddenly laughed. “I take it you’ve been to see Gretchen, then. How did that go?”

“Let’s just say she was far more pleased to see the horses she had loaned us than she was to see me.”

“Have you told her?”

“About our visit with the vampires? That would cost me what little credibility still remains.” Wellington stood and looked toward the door, slightly uncomfortable with the current conversation. “I told her we had been attacked on the road, and that the general and his men rescued us.”

“Did she mention Christine?” Van Helsing was surprised at how dry his mouth suddenly seemed as he asked the question.

“She said Chris has kept pretty much to herself since the last night the two of you were together.”

Van Helsing's blue-grey eyes glistened like polished steel. "When this is over, things are going to be different. I should have listened to her; I *have* wasted too many opportunities."

Wellington gave him an encouraging smile. "Why don't you visit her at the Academy?"

"No," Van Helsing said, shaking his head. "Not yet, at any rate." Looking at Wellington, he smiled. "After that night at the opera, I might be safer with Carmilla."

"It is nothing to joke about," a stern voice reprimanded.

Startled, the two students looked up to see General Spielsdorf standing in the doorway. Behind him stood Major Arcana and a man Van Helsing did not recognize. The general approached and, with his massive hand taking Van Helsing by the jaw, turned the young man's head so as to better study the wounds on his throat. Looking from the punctures, Spielsdorf met Van Helsing's gaze and said, "My boy, you carry an infection far more deadly than any plague. If you should die before Carmilla can be found and destroyed, you will become the same demonic parasite she is…an angel of blood. Only her death will free you from this curse."

"What about exorcism?" Van Helsing asked. "Wouldn't the ancient rite free me from her influence?"

"Would that you could be cured so conveniently," Spielsdorf said, turning to stare at the face of Carmilla in the portrait. "But this pestilence is both physical and spiritual in nature." Turning to Arcana and the stranger, who still stood in the doorway, the general motioned them in.

Arcana positioned himself at the foot of Van Helsing's bed, almost instinctively seeking out a spot that gave him the best overview of his surroundings. The stranger, whose gaze never wavered from the portrait, immediately approached the painting and bent to examine the brushwork. As he studied it, Van Helsing studied him. In spite of the man's silver hair and gold spectacles his face betrayed no particular age, the creases of the browned skin appearing to come from exposure to the elements rather than the passage of time.

Noticing the young man's interest in the newcomer, Spielsdorf said, "This is Baron Vordenburg, from the University of Olomouc, in Moravia. He is, perhaps, the only living authority on the Karnstein family." The baron glanced at Van Helsing and gave a brief nod of greeting, and then returned his attention to the canvas. "Is this the one?" the general asked.

"Yes," the baron said, standing upright. "I had hoped to never look upon that face again."

Van Helsing was surprised by his comment. "You've met Carmilla?"

Baron Vordenburg smiled. "No, thankfully. The girl you call Carmilla is actually Mircalla, the last Countess Karnstein." The baron tapped a corner of the painting, indicating tiny golden script that bore her name and title, beneath which was listed the year A.D. 1698. "This was painted by one of my ancestors, who was, at that time, her lover. They met while both were students at the Scholomance, an academy of the occult hidden in the mountains over what was once known as Lake Hermanstadt. The family legend says the portrait was done with paints into which her blood had been mixed."

"Why?" Van Helsing asked.

"The belief was that such an act would link the portrait to the person, allowing the subject to see what it sees and hear what it hears."

Wellington shook his head. "You don't believe that, do you?"

Vordenburg shrugged. "I can neither prove nor disprove. But if there are such things as the *nosferatu*, who can say what is fact and what is only fiction?"

"Nosferatu?" Van Helsing and Wellington exchanged a glance, each hoping the other would be more knowledgeable.

"Not dead or, more accurately, undead," Spielsdorf explained. "The vampire is the only legend found in one form or another in every known culture, and has many names."

"As does Countess Karnstein," Vordenburg observed. "But there appear to be certain limitations which govern the vampire's actions, extending even to each alias. Note the name Carmilla, an anagram of her true name. Down through the ages she has also been known to present herself as Millarca and Marcilla, both of which are but a rearrangement of 'Mircalla.' These are unusual names in this day and age; perhaps that may help you to find her."

"Yes, if she's registered at a hotel," Spielsdorf said, trying to keep his impatience in check.

Wellington made no attempt at concealing his contempt. "What makes the lot of you think she is still in this region? She knows you are on to her; she's hardly going to wait around until you succeed in sending her to some celestial family reunion with those other two."

"She dares not return to Styria," Spielsdorf replied, sensing a kindred spirit in the young man's outburst. "And she cannot return to the castle after Father Florescu sealed it with the sacraments."

Arcana nodded. "She will stay in self-exile until she feels it is safe to show herself again. But if we can determine where she's sought sanctuary…."

"Why seek her out when she will seek you?" Vordenburg asked. "You have something she wants."

Van Helsing's eyes narrowed. "Meaning me."

"You are bound to her by blood." Vordenburg took off his spectacles and began to wipe the lenses with a handkerchief. "It will be hard for her to release you at this point, especially when your will is low and her lust is up. The vampire is like an addict, consumed by thirst and passion. I understand you are a virgin?"

"I…." Van Helsing found himself unable to answer at the bluntness of the question, and he felt the blood rush to his cheeks.

"No need to be embarrassed," Vordenburg reassured him. "You are among friends here."

"I'm not so sure," Van Helsing said as he shot a hard look at Wellington, knowing he was the only source of such information.

Vordenburg appeared oblivious to Van Helsing's increasing discomfort as he continued. "Untainted blood has long been held to contain mystical properties. In this enlightened age we ignore the folklore of our ancestors, dismissing their wisdom as simple superstition. Such misplaced self-assurance allows the vampire to move about unsuspected and undetected. Yet the vampire is historically attracted to the blood of virgins, which increases their power and restores their youth, implying there is some difference at a basic chemical level that our modern science has yet to discover."

Replacing his spectacles on the bridge of his nose, Vordenburg looked almost longingly at Carmilla's image. "I hope your discipline is as strong as your sword arm, General Spielsdorf. Many years ago that painting came briefly into my possession. I tried to destroy it, but was unable to go through with my plans. It was as if *she* were looking out at me from the canvas, willing me to stay my hand. Soon after that, a man came to claim the portrait and I did not dare refuse because I knew who had sent him and that he would return it to her."

"It will be destroyed," Spielsdorf reassured him, "but only after I have used it to test my theory."

"Then God be with you, for I will not." Vordenburg turned to leave, but paused to add, "Once you open that doorway, you may find it difficult to close again."

"What doorway?" Van Helsing asked as Arcana accompanied Vordenburg out of the room.

"The doorway to the mind," Spielsdorf said, lifting the portrait from its resting place, "or possibly the soul."

*

At General Spielsdorf's urging, Wellington took Van Helsing around the town for the duration of the day, only returning to the hotel early in the evening to join the general, Major Arcana, Father Florescu and Dr. Paole for dinner. Spielsdorf's suggestion had been designed to serve several purposes. Getting Van Helsing back on his feet, out and about among familiar places, would benefit both his metabolism and his morale. It would also insure his weariness after their meal, which Spielsdorf hoped would make him a more suitable subject for hypnosis.

Returning to their rooms from the hotel restaurant, Van Helsing found Spielsdorf had rearranged the furniture in his study. On the general's desk stood the painting of Carmilla, flanked on either side by unlit candles. Arranged in a semi-circle in front of the desk were four chairs, with a fifth chair positioned directly before the portrait. To one side of that chair was another, angled so that whoever occupied it could easily divide his attention between the painting and the spectators.

Van Helsing let out a quiet little laugh at the sight. "Theatre in the round, or Punch and Judy?"

"Almost looks like the set-up for a séance," Wellington said.

"Mesmerism, not spiritualism," Spielsdorf corrected him. "Over time, the vampire can manipulate the mind of its victim, summoning the individual to their side. As such a link is forged between Bram and Carmilla, I want to see if we can use that psychic bridge to cross into her thoughts and find some clue to her whereabouts."

As Wellington, Arcana, Florescu and Paole took their seats in the semi-circle, Spielsdorf motioned for Van Helsing to sit before the portrait. The general darkened the room except for one candle, and then positioned himself in the chair near Van Helsing and the painting. Holding the candle out so that it was directly between Van Helsing and the image of Carmilla, Spielsdorf spoke quietly. "Bram, I want you to fix your gaze on the candle, shutting out everything else around you. Just sit back and relax…look at the light and clear your mind. Take a deep breath, then slowly let it out…another deep breath, then slowly let it out. Start at your feet, and just let the muscles relax…keep breathing, long and slow. Now your legs, let the muscles relax…just let the cares of the day ease away. Just keep focused on the flame and allow the muscles of your hands to relax…long slow breaths…now your arms, let your limbs go limp as if your muscles were melting. There is no tension, there are no worries…."

The general's tone was soft and comforting. Van Helsing felt as if he were floating, adrift on a dark ocean with fog all around. It was as if his body slept while his senses remained alert. He was barely conscious of someone whispering to him from across a great distance, a voice that he could barely make out yet realized it belonged to Spielsdorf.

"…you will remain like this until I awaken you by counting to three. I am going to continue to speak to you, but do not make an effort to listen. Just concentrate on the light and let my words drift into you."

Spielsdorf quietly rose from his chair and used the candle in his hand to light a candle on each side of Carmilla's portrait, then extinguished the flame of his own wick to keep Van Helsing's attention fixed upon the picture as he moved away. The student was barely conscious of the general as the officer stood behind him. Bleary-eyed, Van Helsing's vision blurred as he watched the flickering flames, shimmering and dancing silently atop the candles. He was vaguely aware of voices in the room, but the words were unclear except for the name "Carmilla," which seemed to have been spoken by Spielsdorf. The twin flames dimmed and for a brief moment the two orbs of light were no longer fire but eyes, *Carmilla's eyes*.

While the room remained unchanged to everyone but Van Helsing, Spielsdorf could sense the young man growing tense. "What is it, Bram? What do you see?"

"Nothing," Van Helsing replied. Although he recognized the voice as his own, he was not aware of having spoke. The hazy candlelight seemed to recede, drifting off into the distance until it was drowned in darkness. Now Van Helsing found his attention drawn to the portrait, the face of which was imbued with a faint glow. The puncture wounds on his throat tingled, as if a soft hand had gently touched them. As he gazed intently at Carmilla's image, he was sure he had seen her eyelids flutter. And then her eyes turned to meet his.

As Van Helsing stiffened, Spielsdorf looked from him to the others in the room and asked in hush tones, "Do any of you notice anything unusual?"

Aracana shook his head. "No, do you?"

"No, yet our young friend here is reacting to something."

"Something *is* different," Father Florescu said, crossing himself. "Can't you feel it? Something or someone has come into the room with us."

Although Van Helsing had not seen the priest make the sign of the cross, he saw Carmilla's eyes narrow at the gesture.

He could no longer hear the conversation of his companions, only distant soothing sounds that reminded him of the sounds he had once heard underwater while swimming as a child. Again Carmilla looked at him from the portrait, and she smiled.

"I was afraid I had lost you, Bram" Carmilla said. "I'm all alone now except for you. Aunt Elizabeth is gone, and so is Elga. Your friends have taken them from me. Do you remember what they did to Elga? She loved you, Bram. I love you, too. Don't let them kill me…don't let them do to me what they did to her. Come to me, protect me and let me love you."

"I…I can't…." His voice was so faint that Van Helsing was not sure if he had spoken the words or merely thought them.

Carmilla's eyes were filled with yearning. "If you cannot come to me, then let me come to you. The others don't have to know. Just tell me how to find you."

Van Helsing fought to clear his thoughts, which had suddenly become cluttered with quick glimpses of the past. There was Elga embracing him, then Carmilla kissing him, followed by Christine telling him goodbye outside the opera. No sooner had Christine come to mind than Van Helsing found himself looking at her, her face replacing that of Carmilla's in the portrait. "Christine?" he whispered.

Unable to see Van Helsing's vision, Spielsdorf was puzzled by the strange name. "Who?" he asked, merely mouthing the word as he turned to Wellington.

"She was his fiancée," Wellington replied, his words barely audible for fear of awakening Van Helsing from his trance.

Christine smiled warmly at Van Helsing, her eyes sparkling with the silent laughter that had been so familiar to him in happier times. "I've missed you, Bram. Shall I come to you tonight?"

"Come to me," Van Helsing whispered.

"What?" Spielsdorf's question seemed to burst into Van Helsing's brain, rousing him from his waking slumber. "You must *never* invite her here!"

Father Florescu was on his feet, dashing holy water across the portrait in the sign of the cross. Almost immediately Christine's features shifted back into those of Carmilla. Only Van Helsing could see the fury in the face of the painting, just as he alone had had an audience with Carmilla that night. He would have been tempted to dismiss the events of the entire evening as just an illusion had it not been for the disembodied voice that now echoed through the room for all to hear.

"You think to hunt the hunter?" Carmilla taunted them. "The very life you would save will be used to lead each of you like lambs to the slaughter!" The candles flared up, and the portrait of the vampire burst into flames. The last thing to be consumed were the eyes, which glared at them with all the hatred of hell.

12. An Unexpected Guest.

"We're closed for the night," Gretchen called over one shoulder at the sound of the tavern door opening. Realizing she had already locked the door, she frowned and turned to confront the newcomer as he replied.

"I'm not a customer."

"Well, well, a second visit from Gerald Wellington in one week. Aren't I the lucky one?" Gretchen's eyes narrowed. "And how did you get in here at this hour?"

"Simple," Wellington said. "I picked the lock."

Gretchen grew even more annoyed, partly at him for his nerve and partly at herself for not being angrier with him than she was. "Teach you that in anatomy class, do they?" Turning away from him she went back to her work, cleaning the remaining glasses left from the evening's customers.

Wellington shrugged. "You never know when a client will stiff you on a fee and you have to take matters into your own hands." Ignoring the fact that she was attempting to ignore him, he sat down at the bar on a stool directly behind her. Looking at her reflection, he caught the quick flash of her eyes as she glanced up at him in the mirror behind the bar. "Of course the skill isn't always a mercenary one. Perhaps the patient isn't able to come to the door and unlock it, so you have to let yourself in to save a life."

Gretchen whipped around, bar towel in one hand and soapy glass in another, accidentally splattering foam across Wellington's face in the process as she snapped, "Well if you're here to save a life tonight, you've got the wrong address; I'm doing just fine."

"I *am* here on a medical matter," Wellington said. "Bram is sick…very sick."

Gretchen studied his face closely. He seemed to be telling the truth, but there was still a trace of suspicion in her voice as she asked, "What's that got to do with you coming here?" Motioning to the bottles along the wall, she added, "We're not exactly the apothecary."

"It's hard to explain…." Wellington's voice trailed off as he tried to decide what, and how, to tell her. "This 'infection' that he has affects both the body and the mind…or the spirit."

"The spirit?" Gretchen was sure she had not heard him correctly. "I thought you didn't believe in anything you couldn't dissect?"

"I've encountered a number of things recently that couldn't be tested in a laboratory. I think I've learned more these last weeks outside the university than I ever did within those hallowed walls."

Gretchen's tone was stern. "Maybe you'd learn more within those walls if you actually spent some time inside them. What's wrong with Bram?"

"His affliction isn't fatal; not yet, at least. But he's starting to lose the will to live, which could accelerate his condition."

"I might have something for melancholia," Gretchen said, looking over the rows of bottles behind her.

"I was thinking more along the lines of a house call. Do you think you could talk Christine into going to see him?"

"Let me see if I'm following your line of thought correctly. You've diagnosed your friend with depression, and your prescription is a visit from the ex-girlfriend? You may know a lot about anatomy, but you know very little about the human heart."

"You're right," Wellington said with a sigh. "I guess I'm acting more out of desperation than anything. I just thought the sight of her would cheer him up. He still loves her, you know."

"I know," Gretchen said softly, kissing him on the forehead. "Your heart's in the right place, even if your head's not." As the barmaid turned to pick up a pair of clean glasses with one hand from the counter behind her, she and Wellington both heard a creak come from the door. The two instinctively glanced into the mirror. The door was shut and neither of them saw anyone. In the mirror, Gretchen's eyes met those of Wellington's reflection. "You did lock it again, didn't you?"

"Don't you trust me?"

"Do you really want an answer?" Gretchen asked. She ran the forefinger of her free hand down along the line of bottles. "Pick your poison."

"You know what they say; 'absinthe' makes the heart grow fonder."

Gretchen tried not to smile, knowing it would only encourage him. "What's on your mind?"

"You, more and more," Wellington replied.

"If I had half a brain, I'd toss you out of here."

"Half a brain, but all heart."

"Don't flatter yourself," Gretchen said. "I hate to drink alone, and just happen to be thirsty."

"That makes two of us," came a girl's voice from behind them.

Startled, Gretchen and Wellington whirled to find a young woman with reddish brown hair and a crimson gown standing in the middle of the tavern. Gretchen glanced back at the mirror running the length of the bar, but the glass showed no one but Wellington and herself in the room.

"Carmilla," Wellington whispered.

"A friend of yours?" Gretchen asked in a tone that made him wonder which woman was the lesser of two evils.

"One of Bram's, actually."

"I made you a promise," Carmilla said, never taking her eyes from Wellington as she approached the couple with a slow, graceful pace. "A promise to finish with you what my aunt started."

Remembering the rosary that General Spielsdorf had given him outside Elga's tomb, Wellington ripped the string of beads and cross from around his neck and thrust it toward Carmilla. The vampire hesitated. A puzzled look came across her face and then she laughed, a harsh laugh made even more unpleasant by the fangs her reaction revealed.

Gently reaching out, her palm held upward, Carmilla allowed the cross to lie flat in her hand. Looking from it to Wellington, she smiled. "This tiny trinket has no meaning for you. To an atheist, it's just a simple piece of jewelry."

Gretchen lunged forward, grabbing Wellington's hand with her own as she cried out, "*In manus tuas, Domine*!"

There was a flash of light from the cross as if it had suddenly been turned into white hot metal, searing into the flesh of Carmilla's palm. She tore her hand away from the rosary, tendrils of smoke trailing from the scorched scar the crucifix had left behind. Carmilla sprang toward the window, but it was the body of a wolf rather than a woman that shattered the glass and vanished into the night.

Wellington looked at Gretchen, his eyes filled with disbelief. "Where did you learn Latin?"

"I do occasionally make it to Mass, thank you very much."

Slipping his free hand over Gretchen's, which still gripped his fist, Wellington kissed the girl on the cheek. "What are your views on matrimony?"

"Is that a proposal?" Gretchen looked from Wellington to the broken window, and then back at him again. "I'm not sure which I should be more concerned about, the saber-toothed temptress or this new you."

*

"Is there something wrong with your sausage, Bram?" General Spielsdorf asked. He and Van Helsing were one of the few remaining breakfast customers in the hotel restaurant, partly due to their late arrival after Van Helsing had overslept and partly due to Van Helsing's apparent lack of appetite as he picked at the food on his plate.

"It seems a bit overcooked this morning."

"Overcooked?" Spielsdorf slashed one of the sausages open with his knife to expose the pinkish tinge of the interior. "If they were cooked any less, that one would be bleeding to death." Although he had not spoken of it to anyone, the general disliked the student's increasing inclination toward raw meat. While they had managed to keep Carmilla away from him, there was little they could do to prevent her influence over him.

Van Helsing avoided looking at Spielsdorf's watery grey eyes as they studied him from beneath those bushy eyebrows. Still using his knife, the general lifted the assaulted sausage from Van Helsing's plate and flipped it into his own mouth. The officer's heavy moustache, which drooped down on either side of his mouth to connect with the massive sideburns, writhed about as he chewed his food. Sitting back in his chair, Spielsdorf regard Van Helsing with half-closed eyes that, coupled with the crow's-feet, gave him a world-weary air. After several seconds of uncomfortable silence, the general finally spoke again. "Think back to when you were in contact with Carmilla under hypnosis; are you sure she gave no clue to her whereabouts?"

"No," Van Helsing said. "Nothing."

"We'll do all we can to guard you against her but, if she should get to you, do you think you could confront her…that is, could you do what must be done?"

"You mean kill her?"

"She's already dead; what's left is a demonic presence that wears the human form the way you would wear a mask, seeking blood to sustain itself and maintain its physical shell. Destroy the host body, and the parasitic spirit can no longer remain in the material world."

"I suppose I could start sleeping with a wooden stake under my pillow."

"There are other ways. A blade or bullet piercing the vampire's heart as it sleeps in its coffin by day will destroy it, as will decapitation or fire. It is when they are at rest that they are most vulnerable. The vampire must return to its coffin at least once every 24 hours. This is usually after feeding, allowing its body to become comatose and better digest the blood it has ingested. In the case of newer converts to vampirism this occurs just before sunrise, as they are unable to endure daylight."

"Gerald said when Countess Bathory was killed she aged rapidly until her body was reduced to dust. Yet when Sandor was destroyed, his corpse remained in the same state we first found it."

"Sandor was a new recruit in the ranks of the undead; he would not have had time to decompose had he died a natural death. Upon its demise, the vampire's body will take on the form it would have normally had at the time of its destruction. Elizabeth Bathory died in 1614, and would have already rotted away in the grave long ago."

Van Helsing pushed his plate away. "I seem to have lost my appetite." There had been a tightening sensation in his mouth that morning, as if internal pressure were being applied to his teeth, and the act of eating was becoming uncomfortable. Even his gums ached. Upon shaving earlier, he had been surprised to notice in the mirror that the tissue around his teeth was swollen and red. That, coupled with his recent lethargy, made Van Helsing wonder if Carmilla's attack on him had left him malnourished and subject to scurvy. While he had remained silent on the subject, Spielsdorf had also noticed the symptoms, but it was not scurvy he suspected as the culprit.

"Thank God," came Wellington's voice over Van Helsing's shoulder. Dropping into the chair next to Van Helsing, he snatched up the last remaining sausage from the plate and greedily gobbled it down. "You did say you were done, didn't you?" Wellington managed to ask, in spite of a mouthful of meat.

"Help yourself," Van Helsing said, glancing over at Spielsdorf to see a rare look of amusement in his eyes. "We could have arranged for a few fatted calves if you would have let us know you were coming."

"I wasn't sure about breakfast," Wellington said, eyeing the silver coffee pot and frowning at finding no spare cup upon the table. "I got in late last night."

"You didn't get in at all last night," Spielsdorf observed.

Wellington's face burned with embarrassment before he finally blurted out, "I got engaged last night."

Van Helsing looked at him, dumbfounded. "Anyone I know?"

Now it was Wellington's turn to be befuddled. "To Gretchen; who else?"

"Gretchen agreed to marry you?" Van Helsing raised a skeptical eyebrow. There had to be some mistake. "You've been drinking."

"No, I'm serious and sober," Wellington insisted. "I asked her to marry me and she said 'Yes.'"

"Then *she's* been drinking."

Wellington smiled. "I've got another surprise for you. Out in the lobby." Van Helsing looked at him questioningly, but his only reply was to "Go see for yourself."

Reluctantly leaving the table as Wellington whispered something to the general, Van Helsing made his way out into the lobby of their hotel. The last time his friend had surprised him it had been with the gift of a parrot that, based upon its vocabulary, had been the former mascot of a bordello. His landlady had been less than amused.

Finding nothing outrageous or suspicious awaiting him, Van Helsing decided Wellington must have left the object in question with the receptionist. He started toward the front desk and was halfway across the lobby when a voice at his elbow said, "Bram?"

Turning, Van Helsing found himself face-to-face with Christine. In spite of the foot traffic around them, and in spite of the past, the two immediately but involuntarily embraced.

*

A long walk and talk took the couple to the steps of the Natural History Museum, which Van Helsing eyed with some suspicion. "You might actually enjoy it," Christine said reassuringly. "Archduke Rainer donated his paleontology collection to the museum a few years ago. They say some dinosaurs were larger than elephants." She shivered at the thought. "Can you imagine an age when monsters roamed the world?"

Van Helsing grew grim. "Unfortunately, I can."

"We don't have to go in…." Christine left the thought unfinished.

"No…I want to." Van Helsing smiled, taking her by the elbow and leading her up the steps to the entrance. "It really doesn't matter what we do, so long as I'm here with you."

Christine hesitated. "Things aren't like they were before, Bram. I'm not sure—"

"Neither am I," Van Helsing replied, cutting her off. "On either point."

They entered in silence, which made the sounds of their footsteps echoing in the main hall of the museum seem almost deafening in contrast. Suddenly feeling self-conscious, Christine decided to ask the question Wellington had refused to answer. "Gerald tells me you've been sick, and that you might still be in danger. What is it, Bram?"

"He shouldn't have told you." Van Helsing's tone was curt. "Is that why you're here? Would you have still come to see me if I'd been well?"

Christine's reply was almost a whisper. "I don't know."

Van Helsing's voice softened. "I'm glad you came, either way. I miss you." Sensing the girl's discomfort, Van Helsing quietly cursed himself and tried to change the subject by saying the first thing that came to mind. "Gerald and Gretchen are engaged."

Christine laughed at the notion and at the less-than-subtle effort he had just made. "I know. It's like watching someone slip while ice-skating; it's humorous, even though it really shouldn't be."

"Do you think it will last?"

"The engagement, or the marriage?"

Van Helsing shrugged. "Either."

"Yes, to both." Christine gave him a playful nudge. "Do you think Gretchen would have agreed unless she were sure?"

"You were right," Van Helsing said, after a moment's pause.

"Which time?" Christine asked with a twinkle in her eye.

"That night at the opera. I've thought a lot about what you said. I know things are different between us now, but give me a chance and I *will* change."

Christine met and held his gaze. "I'll make you a deal; I am willing to remain open-minded about us until you've been reinstated at university to continue your studies. But my decision about our future will be based on how you apply yourself, both in and out of the classroom."

Van Helsing smiled. "Fair enough."

"Probably more than fair." Christine kissed him on the cheek.

*

The sky was beginning to grow dark by the time Christine returned to the academy. She had promised Frau Snell she would be back in time for dinner, and had just enough time to freshen up before the meal. Going to her room, she slipped off her coat. Draping it across one arm, she turned up the lamp on her desk and was surprised to find Carmilla sitting in the nearby chair, waiting for her.

"You were gone a long time," Carmilla said. "I missed you." Seeing Christine's guilty smile, a wistful look came into Carmilla's eyes. "You were with *him*, weren't you? I think you still care for him."

Christine blushed and looked down. "He's been very ill."

"Nothing serious I hope?"

"No, I don't think so." Christine looked up, touched by the concern in Carmilla's voice. "This may sound strange, but I think whatever he's going through has done him some good. He seems more reflective, more introspective…I think there's been quite a change in him."

"Yes." Carmilla smiled. "I wouldn't be a bit surprised."

Wincing slightly, Christine tenderly touched her throat.

"Does it still hurt?" Carmilla asked. She rose to her feet and gently undid Christine's collar to reveal the two puncture wounds near the base of her neck. Their jagged edges were inflamed, and stood in sharp relief against her pale flesh. "Here," Carmilla whispered. "Let me kiss it better."

13. Restless Reflections.

"Ouch!" Van Helsing swore beneath his breath as he nicked himself with the razor. Dropping the blade into the washbasin, his hand froze in mid-gesture as he reached for some sticking plaster to stop the bleeding. In the mirror he saw the cut close over and heal itself. Retrieving the razor, he held his free hand up and deliberately sliced his empty palm. Barely had blood started oozing out when the wound sealed shut. His condition was growing worse.

After escorting Christine back to the academy earlier that week, Van Helsing had noticed his night vision vastly improved, penetrating deeper into the darkness without the aid of illumination. Even his hearing had become enhanced, allowing him to hear whispers through the wall. And then there was the oral abnormality. At first he thought his gums were starting to pull back from his teeth, but a closer inspection revealed this was just an illusion caused by the gradual extension of his cuspids. While he had been able to hide that from his companions, there had been no way to cover his increasing pallor.

Leaving his room, Van Helsing found Wellington, Major Arcana and General Spielsdorf clustered about the general's desk. "I've sent down for breakfast this morning," Spielsdorf explained in answer to Van Helsing's inquiring look. "We've things to discuss that would be better unheard by other ears."

As Van Helsing sat down to join them in the wait for room service, he was acutely aware the general was studying him intently for any sign of change. Noticing the look of realization on Van Helsing's face, Spielsdorf abruptly stopped his silent inspection. "Do not despair, my young friend; our battle is not lost, but only beginning. There *is* cause for concern. Wellington's encounter with Carmilla confirms she is here in Buda-Pest, which is a mixed blessing. It means she is close at hand, which narrows our search to this city, but it also means she has a purpose…to claim you for her own."

"Buda-Pest is no crossroad village," Van Helsing observed. "Even if she remains in this area, finding her won't be easy."

Spielsdorf gave him a reassuring smile. "Even in such a city as this, she can find only limited sanctuary. We know she fled Bathory's estate with but one coffin, and it is to that one single coffin she must ultimately return."

Van Helsing nodded. "The legends say the vampire must sleep in its native soil or earth taken from its grave. But where would she hide something as conspicuous as a coffin?"

"Oh Lord," Wellington said. "It could be tucked away in any one of a thousand basements or attics!"

Arcana shook his head. "No. A vampire may only enter a house after first being invited freely by someone who resides there. It's not like an unwanted cousin showing up on your doorstep with their luggage and you have an obligation to let them stay."

"But once they *have* been invited, they can come and go at will," Spielsdorf reminded him. "The vampire can also seek refuge in unhallowed ground, such as a desanctified churchyard or the grave of a suicide. It will be like hunting for the proverbial needle in a haystack, but we benefit in that our 'needle' will be hunting for us with the same passion that we hunt for her."

"Hopefully we find her first," Wellington said.

It doesn't matter who finds who, so long as we are the better prepared when our paths cross," Arcana replied.

"Quite," Spielsdorf said with a nod. "And information may be the most important weapon in our arsenal. The vampire is an unnatural creature; as such, it is in conflict with nature. As Bram here discovered at Bathory's estate, vampires cast no reflection or shadow. Nor can they cross running water under their own power, but must be conveyed via carriage across a bridge or by ship across the waves. Yet there are some aspects of nature these things can control, influencing the elements to summon storms or commanding predatory animals and nocturnal beasts. And they can even assume the form of certain animals, such as the wolf or bat or moth."

"I've seen them dissolve into mist," Van Helsing said.

"Yes, they can dematerialize." Arcana leaned forward, looking Van Helsing directly in the eye. "But keep in mind their supernatural abilities are almost matched by their sheer physical power. The vampire has the strength of many men, imbued with the life force of their victims' blood. Carmilla may look like a mere girl, but she is still a formidable foe even without the use of magic."

Wellington looked over at Van Helsing. "Sounds like the deck's stacked against us this time."

"We are not without trump cards against the vampire," Spielsdorf said. "They are repelled by religious relics and the sacraments, as well as the branches of the wild rose, from which Christ's crown of thorns was woven. And there are certain plants and herbs, such as garlic or onion or even the humble mustard seed, which will prevent their passage."

"I know about the historical use of medicinal herbs," Van Helsing said. "But what is it about these particular plants that vampires fear?"

Spielsdorf shrugged. "It is hard to sift fact from folklore. Many cultures have herbs sacred to their religions. Perhaps there are other plants equally effective against the undead…we have only taken the first few steps in developing a science out of such superstitions, and we still have much to learn."

"Garlic and onion." Wellington shuddered. "Those will keep more than just the vampires away."

A knock at the door announced the arrival of their meal. Barely had the pair of hotel staff started to set up when a second knock sounded and the door was thrown open before anyone could respond. Father Florescu stood in the doorway, his eyes worriedly searching the room.

"You're just in time to join us for…." Spielsdorf's voice trailed off as he noticed the expression on the priest's face. "What is it, Father?"

"Dr. Paole; is he here?" Florescu asked.

Spielsdorf and Arcana exchanged a glance before the general replied. "No, I've not seen him since yesterday. Why?"

"We were to meet this morning, but he never arrived and he never sent word that he would be delayed."

"He may have been called away on an emergency," Van Helsing said. "An occupational hazard for a medical man."

"I'd thought of that," Florescu said with a nod. "But his servants tell me he never returned last night."

"It could still be a professional obligation," Wellington pointed out. "Have you checked the hospital to see if he had been called in to consult on a case?"

Relief filled Florescu's face. "No, I'd not thought of that. Given what we are dealing with, I fear I suspected something sinister."

Their work finished, the hotel servants took their leave. General Spielsdorf was about to speak when yet another rap-tap-tap at the door silenced him. Opening the door, he found the hotel's concierge standing in the hallway with a parcel in his hands.

"I have a package for Abraham Van Helsing," the concierge explained. "I was told I would find him here."

"I'm Van Helsing," the student said, standing.

Spielsdorf took the parcel from the concierge and, after giving him a gratuity, shut the door behind the employee before handing over the bundle to its intended recipient.

"It's not quite Christmas," Van Helsing said, shaking the package in hopes of identifying the contents by sound.

"From Christine?" Wellington asked.

Van Helsing glanced at the top of the package. "It doesn't say."

"There's a note tucked into the wrapping paper," Spielsdorf observed.

Sitting the box on the table, Van Helsing opened the envelope and read its contents, frowning slightly before reading it aloud. "'The perfect gift for an anatomy student. Remember that mine already belongs to you.'" He set the letter aside and opened the package, only to quickly shut it and shove it away. "It's a heart!" Van Helsing gasped, trying not to retch. "A human heart!"

"I'd bet my good eye it belonged to our missing physician," Arcana said, giving a knowing look at Spielsdorf as Father Florescu crossed himself.

"A message from Carmilla," Spielsdorf said grimly, "letting us know she knows where we are."

"She said she would use me to get to each of you," Van Helsing said. "Yesterday afternoon I went to Dr. Paole, to see if he would take another sample of my blood. Carmilla must have followed me and I led her straight to him."

"A sample of blood?" Wellington asked.

"I've been keeping track of the changes under the microscope." Van Helsing was silent for a moment, and then looked at General Spielsdorf as he pulled his lips away from his teeth to show the elongated canines. "I'm becoming more and more like her."

"No, Bram; not like her. Carmilla was no victim; she sought out this existence."

Van Helsing shook his head. "It doesn't matter the path taken, the destination remains the same."

"You have yet to reach that destination, my young friend." Spielsdorf gestured to the breakfast before them. "Come, let us eat. We can plan better on a full stomach."

The very sight and smell of the food made Van Helsing's insides knot up. "I'm not hungry…I'm hardly ever hungry. There's just this thirst that no amount of water or wine ever quenches."

Van Helsing grabbed his cloak from a nearby chair and started to leave. The door was halfway open when he felt a hand on his arm to stop him. Whirling at the interruption, his eyes glowed like live coals as he found himself face-to-face with Wellington.

Almost immediately the hellish light faded from them as his friend stepped back in alarm. Before anyone had a chance to say or do anything Van Helsing rushed from the room, dashing down the hallway to the staircase. Wellington started to go after him, but was stopped by Spielsdorf's sonorous voice.

"Let him go, Gerald. During the daylight hours Carmilla's influence will be weak. He needs to be alone for a while and the cold air will help to clear his mind. Unlike most victims of the vampire, he is aware of what is happening to him. It is a heavy burden to bear, but it may allow him to be on guard against any unusual urges."

Father Florescu shook his head. "I admit I've not had the experience you have had with these creatures, but shouldn't someone at least follow him?"

"Florescu has a point," Arcana said. "If Carmilla retains some form of psychic connection to the boy, she might try to arrange a rendezvous with him while he's away from us."

Spielsdorf thought for a moment, and then nodded. "Go after him, Arcana, but keep out of sight. If he knows you are nearby, then Carmilla might know it as well."

*

Van Helsing's wandering took no particular path, but became a walking tour of random memories as he found himself drawn to places from his past. After roaming the grounds of the university, the collar of his cloak turned up to hide his face in case he encountered any former classmates, he found himself strolling along streets usually only visited after dark. Although he passed many a familiar tavern, he avoided looking in the windows for fear of seeing—or being greeted by—acquaintances. During the course of the last week he had found himself less and less inclined to spend time with others, growing agitated and restless within a matter of minutes during a conversation.

Eventually Van Helsing's steps turned toward Batthyany-erdo, where more than one dawn had seen students' sabers cross over the love of a lady. Ironically, more than one duel had shown more passion than the actual romance that had inspired the conflict. (After one such skirmish, the object of desire eloped with one of the seconds.) The park looked desolate now, the dark bark of the trees glistening with a glaze of ice on bare branches that clawed at the grey skies.

Pausing at the edge of a frozen pond, Van Helsing tested the icy surface with the heel of his boot to determine if it might take his weight as he listened for the sounds of the one who followed him. Although he had yet to determine the identity, Van Helsing's acute hearing had picked up the sounds of distant footsteps upon entering the park. How long he had been followed he could not say, as there had been too many sounds in the city for him to detect an unseen companion earlier. Then came the female voice behind him.

"It's thick enough to skate upon, if that's your fancy."

Van Helsing turned and was surprised to find himself being addressed by a girl with emerald green eyes and copper-colored curls. Her cloak, while not threadbare, had seen better days. Although she wore more make-up than was necessary, he found the effect not unattractive.

"Were you expecting someone else?" she asked, looking about to make sure no one was approaching. "I wouldn't want to interrupt a tryst."

"No, I…." Van Helsing's voice trailed off and his eyes narrowed in suspicion. "Why are you following me?"

"I was coming out of the Golden Peacock as you walked by." The girl shrugged. "I liked what I saw…and you looked lonely. I'm Schnaufen."

"That's an unusual name," Van Helsing said.

"I'm an unusual girl." Schnaufen adjusted the collar of her cloak, carefully but casually allowing it to open enough to give Van Helsing a glimpse of ample bosom. "You still haven't told me your name.

"Van Helsing," he said, trying to appear nonchalant. "Abraham Van Helsing. My friends call me Bram."

"I can be *very* friendly, Bram." Van Helsing stared at the vein at the base of her throat, noticing how it quivered with each beat of her heart. Believing it was a slightly lower part of her anatomy that had attracted his attention, Schnaufen smiled. Stepping forward, she whispered "Very friendly indeed" just before kissing him. Her smile widened and she tilted her head back as he caressed her jawline with a series of short kisses before his mouth moved down to gently graze the tender flesh of her throat. Suddenly the girl found herself yanked away from her potential customer, landing unceremoniously upon her derrière in the snow as Major Arcana confronted Van Helsing.

"You young fool, what are you doing?" Arcana demanded.

"Who's this, your father?" Schnaufen asked, indignant at the interruption.

Arcana turned on her. "If I were *your* father, I'd have you across my knee for a good spanking."

"That costs extra," Schnaufen replied.

As Arcana drew his saber, Schnaufen scrambled to her feet and went scurrying off with a yelp. The major returned the blade to its sheath, trying to hide his amusement. Remembering Van Helsing, all traces of humor quickly vanished. Turning to the student, Arcana grew grim. "I wasn't aware your agenda for this afternoon included tea and strumpets."

Van Helsing's tone was defensive. "*She* kissed me."

“Don’t you understand the danger? You were infected with vampirism by Carmilla’s blood. How do you know exposure to another bodily fluid won’t spread the contagion? As a medical man, can you say with certainty that if any saliva was exchanged between the two of you during a kiss she’s not at risk?” Arcana turned to look off in the direction Schnaufen had disappeared. “A kiss from you could curse her, condemning her to become one of the undead. And there’s an even greater danger to yourself.” Arcana glanced back at Van Helsing and winked. “The wrath of Christine if she catches you with another woman.”

“I….” Van Helsing’s voice trailed off and he felt his cheeks burn with embarrassment.

“I know,” Arcana said sympathetically, “that wasn’t lust I saw in your eyes; it was hunger. But try explaining the differences between an adulterer and a vampire to a jealous woman, and see how quickly she starts lobbing pots and pans and various other household items at your head.”

"The voice of experience?" Van Helsing asked.

Arcana pointed to his eye patch. "How do you think I lost this?"

Van Helsing started to reply but stopped as he felt something brush across his legs. Looking down, he found a large dark cat rubbing itself against him. As the two made eye contact, the bulky beast purred and pressed itself more firmly against his boots. “Well, who do you belong to?” the student asked.

“You do seem popular with felines,” Arcana observed. The cat glared at the officer as he hoisted it up for a better look before handing it to Van Helsing. “You should be safer with this one. In fact, it might even help you find favor with Christine.”

Van Helsing laughed. “He would make the perfect present.”

"Look again," Arcana said. "*She* will make the perfect present."

It was late afternoon when Arcana and Van Helsing, carrying a hefty armload of cat, returned to the hotel. Barely had Van Helsing stepped across the threshold when the cat sprang from his arms and landed on the pavement outside, where it stood staring at him. "Was it something I said?" Van Helsing asked, exchanging a glance with Arcana.

"Maybe it doesn't like being indoors," Arcana suggested, stepping inside the lobby.

Van Helsing hesitated in the doorway, still looking at the animal. "Well, make up your mind. Come in if you're planning on staying."

At that the cat rushed forward to join the two men, following close at their heels as they made their way across the lobby and started up the stairs to their rooms. Upon spotting this new guest, the concierge gave Van Helsing a questioning look. The student stopped to scoop up the cat and reassured the staff member that, "She's only a temporary guest. It's a gift for my girlfriend."

"I'll send up a saucer of milk," the concierge said, adding beneath his breath, "At least it's not one of those little lap dogs, yapping away at all hours of the day and night."

Upon reaching their rooms the cat quickly commandeered the settee for itself. Shaking his head at the sight, Van Helsing slipped off his cloak and started to drape it across the back of one chair when he spotted a note on the mantel. "Here, it's addressed to you," he said to Arcana as he handed him the paper.

"It's from General Spielsdorf," Arcana said. "He and Father Florescu and your friend Wellington seem to be spending the day making the rounds of the various undertakers to see if they can find a lead to where Carmilla may have hidden her coffin."

"Why would she need the aid of an undertaker?"

"Where would be the best place to conceal a coffin? Among other coffins! If Carmilla were to arrange for her coffin to be entered into a vault or mausoleum that has fallen into disuse, its presence would attract little or no attention. She would only need to present herself as the last of that family's line, come to bury a distant relative. It's simply a matter of the fee and a few formalities to insure herself sanctuary."

"Then we can finally run her to ground!" Van Helsing exclaimed.

"I don't want to raise your hopes only to dash them, but keep in mind that it's just one possibility…but I think it's a strong one. It would certainly be the most strategic move our adversary could make."

Dejected, Van Helsing sat on the settee. The cat curled up into his lap. "And if she outwits us?"

"The main thing is to keep you alive. As long as you live, you have a chance. Which means keeping both your strength and your spirits up. Even if you no longer have an appetite, you have to make yourself eat on a regular basis as you normally would. Speaking of which, I seem to recall neither of us had lunch."

Van Helsing glanced at the clock on the mantel. "A bit late for lunch, now."

"And a bit too early for dinner, but I think I can arrange for *something* to be sent up to us. You wait here while I see to that, in case the others come back." Arcana nodded to the cat. "I'm sure she'll see to it you don't get lonely."

As the door closed behind Arcana the cat rolled over on its back, paws up. Van Helsing stood, cradling the creature in one arm and stroking it under the chin as he went into his bedroom. "Don't you look regal?" he said at the contented look in the animal's eyes. "I think I'll call you Duchess."

"Countess," a familiar voice corrected him as the body of the cat expanded and shifted until Van Helsing found it was Carmilla he carried in his arms. "If anyone sees us like this, they'll think we're on our honeymoon."

"Away with you, wench!" Van Helsing tossed Carmilla onto his bed.

"Wench?" Carmilla repeated in mock shock. "Is that any way to talk to the woman who loves you?"

"Love? You don't know what the word means."

"That's not true." Carmilla pretended to pout. "Didn't you get my Valentine?"

"We're just into December; a bit early for Valentine's Day, don't you think?"

Carmilla smiled. "Time has no meaning for us."

"*Life* has no meaning for your kind."

This time Carmilla's injured tone was not feigned. "*My* kind? You condemn me for wanting to survive? How many animals have died to sustain *you*, given their very lives so that you could live? Do you criticize the cat for eating the rat, or the wolf when it brings down a stag, or the fox for feeding upon the fowl? Should the hare take up arms against you for hunting it?"

Van Helsing felt suddenly tired. "Those are victims without souls," he said, sinking into a nearby chair before his legs could buckle beneath him.

Carmilla laughed, a harsh and hideous laugh that made Van Helsing wince to hear it. "So you admit they are beneath you in the grand scheme of things." Slowly she slipped from the bed and strolled toward him. Remembering his rosary on the nightstand, Van Helsing tried to spring from his chair and grab it, only to find himself paralyzed. Lifting the front of her skirts, Carmilla eased herself onto Van Helsing's lap and whispered, "Join me, and you will be elevated to an existence that places you as much above humans as humans are above animals."

Even Van Helsing's voice failed him as he tried to reply. Carmilla had taken total control over him. Again he glanced toward the rosary and she followed his gaze. "Is that for me?" she asked in taunting tones. "How thoughtful." Kissing the tip of his nose, Carmilla rose and released her hold over him. Gesturing toward the rosary, she nodded at the nightstand. "Go on; I won't stop you."

Van Helsing warily got to his feet, his eyes never leaving Carmilla as he made his way to the tiny table by his bed. Still watching her, he reached for the rosary, only to fling it away with a scream as its touch scorched his palm and fingers.

"Does it hurt much?" Carmilla asked innocently. Going to his side, she took his hand in hers and gently kissed the blistered flesh. "Come here, let me show you something."

Leading him to the nearby washstand, with her free hand Carmilla pointed to the oval mirror mounted over the marble basin. Van Helsing looked into the glass, finding the room reflected clearly where Carmilla's image should have been seen. And then he realized that she was pointing to a particular section of the mirror, at his face, and felt his heart skip a beat. His reflection was faint, almost transparent, allowing him to see the dim outline of the room behind him. Carmilla pressed her lips to his ear and spoke softly. "You see; you and I are not so different after all."

Raising his wrist to her mouth, Carmilla bit into it and began to drink. Between the shock of what he had seen and the loss of blood, Van Helsing sank to his knees, his eyes glassing over as Carmilla caught him and eased his body to the floor. She was just about to resume feeding when she heard sounds from the outer room and sprang toward the door like a panther about to pounce upon its prey.

"Bram?" Arcana called.

As the major stuck his head inside the bedroom to check on Van Helsing, Carmilla's hand clamped about his throat, crushing his windpipe. "Shhh," she whispered, still clutching Arcana in her vice-like grip as she raised a cautioning finger to her lips. "You'll wake him and he needs his rest."

Arcana's fists gripped Carmilla's wrist, but he was unable to break her grasp. Choking, he still struggled to free himself as she waltzed him across the room to burst through the glass doors that led out to the balcony, sending a shower of shattered glass down into the street below. Gloating as Arcana collapsed in her arms, Carmilla's triumph was short-lived. Shouts from the street at the sounds of their struggle attracted her attention, and she spotted General Spielsdorf and Father Florescu dashing across the frozen cobblestones toward the hotel. Hurling Arcana's corpse at her would-be adversaries, Carmilla sprang from the balcony, her body dissolving into mist to drift away on cold currents of air.

14. Tragedy in Triumph.

Suddenly conscious, Van Helsing bolted upright in his bed, only to find the room swirling around him. His mouth dry, every beat of his heart produced a pounding in his temples. He managed to make out Gerald Wellington standing near him before he fell back, his head hitting the pillow with a muffled *thumpf.*

"Have I been drinking?" Van Helsing asked hoarsely.

"No, but your friend Carmilla has," Wellington replied. "A nightcap with her is as deadly as nightshade."

"You must not sit up too quickly," General Spielsdorf said, coming into Van Helsing's bedroom at the sound of the two men talking. "You've lost a considerable amount of blood. Fortunately, your friend here arrived in time for us to perform a transfusion."

"Consider it a loan," Wellington said.

"I've got *your* blood flowing through my veins?" Van Helsing asked. "No wonder I feel hungover." He paused and frowned as dim memories came back to him. "The major…?"

Growing grim, Spielsdorf shook his head. "Major Arcana is dead. Carmilla not only knows where we are, but has managed to be invited into the hotel by someone in residence here. That means she can now come and go as she pleases. I've rubbed garlic around the doorways and windows of our rooms; that will at least keep you safe within these walls. But we must take extra precautions should any of us venture outside our own chambers." The general took the rosary from Van Helsing's nightstand, saying, "As long as Carmilla walks, you must never be without this."

Van Helsing trembled at the sight of it. "I can't take that…I can't even touch it." Holding up his hand, he showed them the burnt flesh of his palm. The wound was a violent contrast to the ashen skin around it. "I tried to use it against Carmilla when she was here last night, but it did as much harm to me as it would have her. Bring me a shaving glass."

As Wellington went to fetch the requested mirror, Spielsdorf studied Van Helsing's face, noting the feverish intensity of his gaze. Even after the blood transfusion, his complexion was still pale. Returning with the glass, Wellington held it out but Van Helsing made no attempt to take it.

"Look at it," Van Helsing said. "Look at *me* in it." Spielsdorf and Wellington leaned in to see the image in the mirror, only to find a faint phantom reflection of Van Helsing in the glass. "How much longer until she and I are one?"

"As long as you are alive, there is hope," Spielsdorf reassured him. "Only in death will the transformation become complete."

Van Helsing sat up, swinging his feet down to the floor as he threw back the covers. "If it's a matter of it being her or me, I can't stay in here like a prisoner or patient."

Spielsdorf's smile was a mixture of patience and sympathy. "I can understand your desperation, but you're too vulnerable to be out and about. Let us deal with this."

"Deal with it?" Van Helsing asked. "Paole is dead. Arcana is dead. Who's next? You? Gerald? Father Florescu? Your numbers are dwindling and time is on her side. What if she goes into hiding and simply waits for me to die of old age? What's the length of a single lifetime to someone immortal like Carmilla? Sooner or later, I *will* die. Whether I become dead or undead depends upon what we do now."

"I know Carmilla better than you," Spielsdorf replied. "This is a game to her. She is playing with us like a cat would a mouse before killing it. And like a cat, she won't just walk away and allow you to die of natural causes."

"And I won't just sit and wait. Carmilla is impulsive; she lives for the moment. We can use that against her. If this is a game to her then let's make it a game of chess; not just thinking about the next move as she does, but also about the moves that will be triggered by that one."

Spielsdorf started to speak but Wellington cut him off. "It's no use, General; I've seen that look in his eye before. Even all of Carmilla's hypnotic power couldn't make him change his mind."

The general was silent for a moment. With a sigh, he shook his head and said, "Very well, but with certain conditions." Removing the dagger he wore hidden under his jacket, Spielsdorf handed it to Van Helsing. "To begin with, you will keep this with you at all times. Even when you are here at the hotel, sleep with it under your pillow. I had that silver blade made in hopes of one day plunging it into Carmilla's dark heart. Secondly, you start eating regularly once more."

"Even if we have to force it down you," Wellington chimed in.

Spielsdorf nodded. "You have to keep your strength up for the fight ahead, and it's important for your body to maintain its normal digestive function. You're not at the point where you can live on a liquid diet like Carmilla."

"Let's at least *start* with some liquids," Van Helsing said. "Coffee…hot as hell and black as night."

Wellington looked crestfallen. "I was thinking more along the lines of Chardonnay and eggs."

Consulting his pocket watch, Spielsdorf shook his head. "At the risk of shattering your dreams of a Champagne breakfast, I feel compelled to point out that it's well after noon. But, given what the two of you have been through, I suppose I cannot complain about your having slept half the day away."

"I've got it!" Wellington exclaimed, snapping his fingers. "We have a late lunch and then spend the afternoon with Gretchen and Christine."

Van Helsing thought the matter over for a moment. "I haven't seen Chris for several days, but after what happened last night—"

"You need something to chase away the doom and gloom," Wellington said, cutting him off. "What is it they taught us to tell our patients? A positive and cheerful disposition aids in the healing process."

"The only thing that's going to heal me is to kill Carmilla."

"For once, Wellington may be right. Fresh air and activity would do you good. It gets the blood flowing and rejuvenates the body. And before I forget," Spielsdorf reached into his pocket and removed a letter, "this arrived for you earlier, Bram. Judging from the hint of cologne, I suspect it comes from Christine."

Taking the envelope, Van Helsing opened it and began to read, pausing as he realized Wellington was looking over his shoulder. "Do you mind?"

Wellington shrugged and stepped away. "Didn't look all that intimate to me."

"It's Christine," Van Helsing said as he continued reading. "She wants me to meet her at Adlerberg this evening after dinner.

"Granted the weather has been a bit warmer this week, but wouldn't spring be a more appropriate season for a rendezvous at the vineyards? Or are you two planning a romantic sleigh ride in the moonlight?"

"Chris and I first met at Adlerberg; it's always been her favorite place. She…." Van Helsing's voice trailed off and he smiled as he finished the letter.

"Yes?" Wellington asked, encouraging him to continue.

Van Helsing looked up, and both Wellington and Spielsdorf were pleased to see color return to his cheeks. "She wants to talk about our future."

"Oh God, another unfortunate fellow condemned to matrimony," Wellington sighed.

"I seem to recall *your* recent engagement," Spielsdorf reminded him.

"That was different," Wellington replied. "It was *my* decision to sacrifice my bachelorhood and become a martyr to amore. But in the hands of a pretty puppeteer, Bram's heartstrings can be used to manipulate him like a marionette."

Van Helsing gave him a withering look. "Given how quickly a pretty face can turn your head, it's a wonder you've not got whiplash."

Spielsdorf went over to the black leather medical case on the nightstand and began digging through its contents. Above the tinkle of metal instruments and glass bottles made by the search, Wellington asked, "Looking for something specific?"

"Tincture of laudanum," Spielsdorf replied. "The two of you are giving me a headache."

*

The roar and crackle of the fire in the hearth, punctuated by the laughter and chatter of the customers, added as much warmth to the atmosphere of the tavern as the flames. As Wellington stepped into the Wolf's Head and slipped the cloak from his shoulders, the smell of food cooking in the kitchen reached him in spite of the pipe smoke spiraling up around him from the nearby tables. Even the very thought of sizzling sausages chased away the chill of the darkening skies. Spotting Gretchen carrying a tray of tankards, Wellington slipped quickly and quietly alongside her and helped himself to one of the pewter mugs.

"And what makes you think any of this ale is for you?" Gretchen asked.

"Because we've reached that point in our relationship where we anticipate each other's needs."

"What you need is a good boot to the backside." Gretchen snatched the tankard away from him before he could decrease its contents by so much as a sip. "Judging from that look in your eye, your hunger isn't confined to food."

Wellington took another tankard from the tray as Gretchen returned the first one to its former spot. "I have time enough for both you and stew. Bram's meeting Christine, so you have me available to you for the entire evening."

"Christine?" Gretchen's eyebrows furrowed as she frowned. "Are you sure?"

"I saw her letter to him before lunch; it was her handwriting."

"I went to the academy this morning to see if Chris wanted to have breakfast. Frau Snell said they haven't seen Christine for three days. Since you'd been away for about that long, I thought you and Bram already knew and had gone looking for her."

Wellington grabbed Gretchen by the arm, yanking her toward the door and sending the tray of tankards crashing and splashing to the floor. "Come on!"

"Where are we going?" Gretchen asked, trying to keep up with him.

"I'm taking you to Father Florescu and then going after Bram. If Carmilla is behind this, he's walking into a trap."

"I can't leave here," Gretchen protested, trying to pull free only to feel Wellington's grip tighten. "I'll lose my job."

"Better that than losing your life. You'll be safer in a basilica than behind a bar."

*

The crisp snow crunched beneath the hooves of Van Helsing's horse as he rode out from beneath the canopy of trees that lined the lane leading to the vineyards. It was the first time he had been there in winter, and the barren vines looked like black lace stretching out over the orchard in the blue/white light of the moon. Even as clouds drifted past the glowing orb in the sky overhead, briefly darkening the landscape, he found he could still see clearly across the field. This dubious benefit of having Carmilla's blood flowing through him furthered his resolve to tell Christine everything that had happened to him at Bathory's estate. She had to know the risk she was sharing with him if they were to stay together.

His horse snorted and reared up, interrupting Van Helsing's reverie. Firmly but gently reining the animal in, he petted its neck reassuringly. "Easy, lad. There's no need to be nervous; the lady doesn't bite."

Barely were the words out of his mouth when a hand grabbed his knee. Christine laughed at the startled expression on his face. "I thought you said there was no need to be nervous?"

Trying to recover his dignity and hoping the moonlight covered his embarrassment, Van Helsing slipped down from his saddle. "You just took ten years off my life. I should take a riding crop to you."

"You don't own a riding crop," Christine reminded him.

"Would you settle for a saber?" Van Helsing asked as he rested one hand on the hilt of his sword. "The flat of the blade is probably just as effective on a delicate derriere."

Christine raised a reprimanding eyebrow. "I'm not sure I care for the turn your anatomical studies seem to have taken. I believe the Hippocratic Oath binds you to heal, not harm, your patients."

Van Helsing slipped his arms around Christine and kissed her, saying, "Fortunately for me our relationship is personal, not professional." Kissing her again, he added, "Of course, having not completed my studies, I've not actually taken the oath yet."

Pressing herself closer to him, her head tucked beneath his chin, Christine whispered, "Oath or no oath, you could never hurt me."

"No," Van Helsing shook his head. "At least not intentionally. But I do have something I feel you need to know, and hearing it may be painful."

"I already know," Christine replied. She tilted her head back to gaze into his eyes. "I know about Elga, and I know about Carmilla." Van Helsing found himself speechless at such an unexpected revelation. Sensing his discomfort, Christine tried to put him at ease. "You're not responsible for what happened. I know what they are, and the kind of power they possess. Remember that night at the theatre? They must have been stalking you even then."

"I can't believe Gretchen told you...." Van Helsing felt his face go flush with embarrassment for a second time that night. "Then again, maybe it's better that you did hear it from her first."

"None of that matters," Christine said reassuringly. Van Helsing studied her face, amazed at her acceptance of the situation. Clutching her closer to him, a wave of emotion swept over him and he felt his eyes start to sting with tears. Her own embrace about him tightened as she said, "The important thing is to stop Carmilla; she's the only obstacle that still stands between us. Now that we're together again, I won't let her or anyone else ever take you away from me."

"If we can find her resting place, we can destroy her." Van Helsing's tone was one of grim desperation. "Spielsdorf has spent years trying to track her down."

"I know where she keeps her coffin," Christine said.

Van Helsing stared at Christine, not sure that he had heard her correctly.

Christine nodded to confirm what she had said. "Carmilla has been posing as a student at the academy."

Van Helsing felt a surge of happiness swell up within him. For the first time in weeks it seemed as if there was a chance of ending the curse that hung over him. "But how did you...?" His voice trailed off as he glanced down at the ground. The clouds had cleared away from the moon, bathing the couple in its pale light. There were no footprints in the snow where Christine had stepped, and only his own faint shadow showed upon the crystalline surface. She had become one of them.

Christine sensed the sudden change that had come over him, feeling his body tense up even through his clothes and cloak. Following his gaze, she understood the discovery he had made. She looked down as a twinge of sadness passed through her, wishing she could have had the chance to tell him herself. Her eyes pleaded as she looked back at him. "You and I are not like her, Bram; we're not like Carmilla or Countess Bathory. We don't have to kill in order to survive, and we need make no more like us. Think about it; to be together forever, never growing old, remaining the same throughout the centuries—"

"We're supposed to change!" Van Helsing said, white-hot tears streaming down his cheeks as he involuntarily pulled away from her. "The living evolve. It's the brevity of life that makes each moment important. Look at Carmilla; easily jaded and constantly bored."

"It's because she has no one to share her existence. Why do you think she wants you?"

"And how long before I'm cast aside with the same casual contempt she has for everything and everyone else? I can't believe you're...." Van Helsing could not finish the thought.

"I'm sorry, Bram; I didn't ask for this."

Van Helsing could taste his tears as he spoke. "I know." Stepping forward, he took her in his arms again and hugged her. "It's not your fault. I can't undo what Carmilla has done to you, but we can make sure she never does this to anyone else. Where is she?"

"Carmilla's coffin is in the attic of the academy. Those rooms are rarely used; the girls are all afraid to go up there for fear of bats." Looking up, Christine gave him a bittersweet smile, the tips of her teeth glistening against her lips. "Who knew just how justified those fears would be?" She struggled to find something else to say, but only a choked "I love you" came out.

"I love you, too," Van Helsing said. He bent his head down to kiss her, his mouth meeting hers as he thrust the silver dagger Spielsdorf had given him deep into her heart. Her dying body started to slip from his arms; her mouth and eyes wide open as realization set in. Never letting her go, Van Helsing eased Christine onto the ground, cradling her head in his lap. The crimson tears that had started to stream from her eyes gradually turned clear as Carmilla's curse was lifted from her.

It began to snow, faint flakes slowly waltzing down around them in silence as an expanding pool of blood spread out around Christine's body like sanguine wings. Van Helsing never took his eyes from her face, not even looking up at the sound of approaching hoofbeats. The horse stopped near them and Van Helsing heard the rider dismount. Gently he caressed Christine's cheek. Only when the newcomer's hand gripped his shoulder did he turn his head to see Gerald Wellington standing over him.

"Bram, I—"

"Take her to Father Florescu," Van Helsing said, starting to stand. Gathering Christine up in his arms, he kissed her one last time and gently handed her to Wellington. "I don't want anyone to see her like this." Turning away, Van Helsing walked toward his horse.

"Where are you going?" Wellington asked.

"To the academy. I have some unfinished business with the Countess Karnstein."

15. Ashes to Ashes, Dust to Dust.

It had taken repeated poundings on the door of the Snell Academy for Young Women before Frau Snell was roused from her bed. As she stood shivering in the doorway, candle in one hand and key ring in the other, she regarded Van Helsing with a mixture of concern and confusion at such a late visit. "Christine isn't here," she began.

"Christine is with God," Van Helsing said, curtly cutting her off as he pushed past the woman and made his way inside. He looked about to see if any of the students were stirring. "Gather the girls and get them out of here."

"What?"

Van Helsing's eyes were ice cold as he met Frau Snell's gaze, and there was a grim firmness to his mouth as he spoke. "Christine died of a diabolical disease. We have to reduce the risk of infection until I am sure the pestilence has been purged from this place."

"But where are we to go at this hour?"

"To a hotel, to a church, anywhere, just take the girls as far away from here as possible." Van Helsing started for the staircase, and then hesitated. Turning back to Frau Snell, he asked, "Is the attic unlocked?"

"Why no, we—"

Van Helsing's hand shot out, palm upward. "May I have the keys, please?"

"What on earth has the attic got to do with all of this?"

"This disease is usually carried by bats. I suspect the cause of Christine's affliction may be found up there." Seeing the distress in Frau Snell's eyes, Van Helsing realized how brusque he had been. "Please?" he repeated softly.

"I…I'm sorry," Frau Snell apologized, handing him the ring of keys. "It's just with everything happening at once, and Christine dead…is it hydrophobia?"

"Would that it *were* just an outbreak of rabies."

Van Helsing took the keys and dashed up the steps, dimly aware of the director following some distance behind him to begin waking the girls. Ignoring her knocks as she rapped on the bedroom doors down on the second floor, Van Helsing jabbed the key into the lock of the attic door and twisted it open with a loud metallic snap. There was no need for stealth; Carmilla was not one to pass the time by idly sitting about some dusty, musty attic. If she were inside, it would only be because she was at rest in her coffin.

Leaving the key in the lock, Van Helsing took the Kukri knife from the sheath on his belt and slowly wove his way through the cobweb-encrusted furniture long ago stored away and forgotten. There were enough pieces scattered about to furnish a small cottage. Barely had the thought flashed through his mind when a flash of gold caught his eye. In the far corner of the attic, Carmilla's coffin rested on the floor, its gilded trim glittering in the moonlight that poured in through the window. Raising the great blade overhead Van Helsing wrenched open the coffin lid, prepared to plunge the Kukri into Carmilla's breast. At the sight of the empty coffin he silently cursed himself as much for his impatience as his optimism.

Returning the knife to its sheath, Van Helsing closed the lid of the coffin. He had but to hide himself away in the academy and wait; Carmilla would eventually return to her resting place and he could kill her as she slept. Leaving the attic, he shut the door and locked it behind him. He must leave no trace of his presence, no sign that would arouse her suspicions.

Van Helsing slipped the key ring into the pocket of his cloak. Barely had he reached the staircase when he noticed a dim, misty spiral in the air before him. Had it not been caught and illuminated in a shaft of moonlight from the domed skylight overhead, it would have gone unnoticed. Initially dismissing it as dust stirred up either by his own activity or the hustle and bustle of the girls' hasty departure, he realized it was growing in density rather than dissipating. A shadowy shape formed, a living silhouette that went from mist to matter as Carmilla materialized at the top of the steps.

"I had no idea we were receiving visitors this evening," Carmilla said, curtseying. "Have you come to see me or Christine?"

"Christine is dead."

"And…you…killed her?" Carmilla smiled. "Why you mad, impetuous lad. And you've sent the rest of the girls away so that we could have the house to ourselves. Does this mean you have finally come to your senses and chosen me over her?"

"Christine is dead," Van Helsing repeated. "True dead. Just like Elga. Just like Elizabeth." Slipping the cloak from his shoulders, he drew both the Kukri knife and his saber from their scabbards. "I think it's time you were reunited with your family."

Carmilla laughed. "Is this where you deliver some Shakespearean speech about avenging the injustices done to you?"

Glancing at the weapons he wielded, she placed her hands on her hips and gave him a reproachful pout. “That hardly seems gallant, drawing a sword on an unarmed opponent.”

“Unarmed? You’re as lethal as a leopard; your whole body is a weapon.”

“A leopard? I didn’t know your tastes ran to the exotic.” Carmilla gave him a playful wink. “Would you settle for something a little more domestic?”

The last word was still on Carmilla’s tongue as she lunged forward, fur replacing flesh as her lithe form became lupine. In spite of his reflexes, the wolf was too fast and too close for Van Helsing to be able to use either blade effectively. Flinging himself to one side, he was just barely able to escape the creature’s jaws as it snapped at his throat. Van Helsing sprang to his feet but the wolf had already recovered and slammed into his chest, sending both opponents tumbling down the steps to crash in a heap upon the landing.

Dazed and breathless, Van Helsing struggled to get up, only to find Carmilla sitting just a few feet away from him on the marble tile, her arms wrapped about her legs with her chin resting on her knees. “Did you miss me?”

Unable to speak, Van Helsing tried to focus. His saber was within arm’s reach, but it would take a moment to gather his energy for the attempt. “That guise is certainly easier on the eyes.” He winced in pain as he sat up. “And on the body.”

Carmilla seemed pleased at the compliment, regardless of its actual intent. “I'm impressed; you appear to be in better shape than I would have imagined, given our last tryst.”

“I believe we discussed the technique of blood transfusion over dinner one evening at your aunt's.”

"So we did." Carmilla thought about the concept. "I took the blood out, and someone else put the blood back in. That makes you a veritable horn-of-plenty."

Van Helsing grabbed the saber and lashed out at Carmilla, slashing her face as she tried to twist away from the oncoming blade. "The dining room is now closed," Van Helsing said, getting to his feet.

Standing, Carmilla ran one hand across her wound, looking at the blood on her fingers before licking them. She shook her head as if trying to patiently correct a child as the gash across her cheek and chin healed itself. "You haven't really thought this through, have you? You and I are so much alike now that you can't even use religious relics against me. You no longer have an advantage."

"After Christine's transformation she still loved me, just as she did in life. Even if you kill me and I become like you, my contempt for you will continue. That gives me an eternity to hunt you down and destroy you, witch."

"Witch? Hypocrite, your own profession has its origins in the occult. If there had been no alchemy, there would be no medicine. I have defeated death; age and disease cannot touch me. The goal of the physician is to prolong life. I have achieved what your science still seeks."

"Same goal, different paths. We care about others; you only care about yourself."

"That's not true," Carmilla said. "I care about you. I could have just drained you and left you to die. Instead I shared my essence with you to insure your survival."

"And what about Christine?" Van Helsing asked. "You shared your blood with her as well. Was it because you loved her, too? No, you simply used her to get to me. We're just pawns on a chessboard to you."

From the corner of her eye Carmilla looked over at the pair of sabers mounted on the wall. "Let's have one final game." Walking slowly to the swords, keeping a sly eye on Van Helsing in case of attack, she removed a weapon from the wall. "Shall we?"

"A duel with Death? I lunge forward to plunge my blade into your black heart, only to find the sword passing through a cloud of mist as you make your escape. What would be the point?"

"No magic," Carmilla promised. "I will remain in this form for the duration of the duel."

Van Helsing made no attempt to hide his suspicions. "What's the catch?"

"No catch, but there are conditions. If I win, you remain with me, giving me your word that you will never betray me or my trust. You've always valued honor, so I know if I have your word on this I can rely upon it."

"I'd rather die."

"Considering your current condition, that's not really an option for you, is it? You claim I show no consideration for others, so now I give you *my* word: Should I win, so long as you keep your commitment to me I will never again kill or convert another human being, but only take enough blood to survive."

"And if I refuse?"

"I will leave here now and you will never see me again. But I swear to you, I will slaughter every living thing you have ever known or loved. Gerald and Gretchen to begin with, and then on to your mother and father before finishing off the rest of your family."

Van Helsing shifted his body, sword coming up as he spoke. "*En garde*!"

Carmilla smiled, gathering up her skirts with her free hand to allow herself more mobility. Saluting Van Helsing with her sword, she prepared for his attack. Barely had she assumed the defensive position when he sprang forward but, in spite of his speed, she deflected his saber with her own. Their blades were a blur in a furiously repeated cycle of thrust, parry and riposte as the sounds of steel slashing and clashing echoed throughout the empty house.

Gradually Van Helsing found himself forced back down the steps that led to the main hall, giving Carmilla the advantage of having the high ground as they descended the staircase. Van Helsing's foot slipped and he started to fall forward. Carmilla pressed the advantage and drove her sword toward him. Anticipating her intent, Van Helsing made no attempt to avoid or slow his fall but used its momentum to drop below her blade, which only grazed his shoulder. Wincing at the pain as his free forearm broke his fall upon the stone steps, he rammed his saber upward into Carmilla before she could recover from her attack. There was a cry of rage and pain from her as she dropped her sword, her body tumbling over his as it rolled down the remaining steps to the floor below.

Wasting no time, Van Helsing was on his feet to grab his opponent's discarded weapon. At the foot of the staircase Carmilla lay face down on the marble floor, and just a few feet from her was the Kukri knife that Van Helsing had dropped during Carmilla's initial attack at the top of the steps. Dashing down the steps and leaping across Carmilla's motionless form, he snatched up the Kukri knife. Turning, he found himself face-to-face with Carmilla, who stood with his sword still protruding from her stomach.

Carmilla grasped the hilt of his sword and slowly pulled it out. "You can't be much of an anatomy student; you seem to have forgotten where my heart is."

"I'm not so sure you have such an organ."

"Oh Bram, you're not going to be a sore loser are you?"

"Don't be too premature in announcing a winner," Van Helsing said, indicating the sword and knife he brandished. "Where did you learn the saber?"

"Apparently old Spielsdorf has been neglecting your education. We acquire your skills as we absorb your blood. We should be well matched, you and I." Carmilla glanced down at her exposed stomach, watching the wound heal. Fingering the torn cloth around the vanishing injury, she looked up at Van Helsing. "*Someone* owes me a new dress."

"Black, for your funeral?"

"White, for our wedding."

"Wedding?" Van Helsing shook his head in disbelief as he turned and slowly walked away from her. "Even if I were willing, what cathedral could either of us ever enter?"

Going into the parlor, Van Helsing knelt before the fireplace and used the tip of his saber to stir up the dying embers. Although Carmilla made no sound as she entered the room, he could still sense her presence. Kneeling beside him, she teasingly tapped his saber with her own. "Don't you want to play anymore?"

Van Helsing tossed the saber aside. Reaching for the nearby poker, he stabbed at the partially burnt logs, rekindling the flames amid a shower of sparks. "I'm cold and I'm tired."

Carmilla kissed his cheek. She took the Kukri knife from him and placed it and her saber on the hearth, and then gently opened his collar to reveal the bruised bite marks on his neck. "Then let me finish it. You'll never feel chilled or weary again."

Van Helsing stared into the fire. "Will I be capable of feeling anything?"

"You told me Christine still loved you after her transformation."

"I could never love you." Van Helsing turned to her as he continued, "And you will never really love me. You're infatuated with me because I'm *not* infatuated with you." Giving a final jab at the flames, he stood. "You want me because you can't have me."

"I *will* have you, one way or the other." Carmilla's jaw clenched, her eyes glistening red in the firelight. "If you think otherwise, you have been sadly misinformed."

Raising the poker up, Van Helsing watched the smoke rise from its iron tip. "The feeling is mutual."

With a quick twist of his wrist Van Helsing flipped the poker around and rammed the barbed tip between Carmilla's shoulder blades, using the weight of his body to drive it down through her heart until it burst through her chest. Carmilla bolted upright and whirled, backhanding Van Helsing with such force that he was thrown against one wall, where he dropped to the floor in a daze. Unaware that the violence of her movement had swept the lower hem of her dress into the fire in the hearth behind her, Carmilla grabbed the poker to tear it out, the moist hiss of the hot iron against her flesh drowned out by her agonized cry as her face became creased with age and her hair grew grey.

By now the back of Carmilla's dress had burst into flames while she still struggled to wrench the shaft from her writhing form. Van Helsing regained his senses and used a nearby table to pull himself to his feet. Grabbing the oil lamp from the table, he hurled it at Carmilla, turning her into a living inferno as it shattered on the floor at her feet. The burning oil spread out in a fiery pool around her. Blindly Carmilla tried to race from the room, igniting furniture and fixtures as she stumbled into them in a vain attempt to reach the main hall.

Recovering his saber and the Kukri knife, Van Helsing approached Carmilla. "It's over."

The blazing figure reached out to him. "Mercy!"

"I'll show you the same mercy you showed to Christine," Van Helsing said, bringing the blade of the Kukri slicing through the air to strike Carmilla's head from her neck.

Carmilla's lifeless body crumpled to the floor and the ancient flesh and bones were quickly consumed. Van Helsing realized the fire had spread too far throughout the room to be extinguished. Reluctantly, with one last look back, he fled with a final image burned into his brain: That of Carmilla's fanged skull glaring at him with empty eye sockets from the center of the room.

*

From the end of the lane Abraham Van Helsing sat in his saddle and watched as the fire finished gutting the stone structure of the academy. The distant horizon was tinged blood red with the rising sun when the sound of hoofbeats greeted his ears. Turning, he saw Gerald Wellington and General Spielsdorf approaching him on horseback.

Pulling up alongside Van Helsing, Spielsdorf looked from the young man to the smoldering remains of the school and then back at him again before asking, "Carmilla?"

Van Helsing nodded toward the academy, and then pulled open his collar to reveal the flesh of his throat had healed. Wellington rested one hand on his friend's shoulder and Van Helsing gave him a weary smile. The expression faded from his lips at the sight of a cloud of smoke rising from the ruins, spreading out upon the morning breeze to take on the appearance of an enormous bat. Then the wind shifted, briefly turning the shape into that of a cross before carrying the scattering cloud away.

"Is it over?" Wellington asked.

"No, it's not over. It will never be over," Van Helsing vowed, tugging on his reins to turn his horse around and ride away. "Not as long as even one of those creatures still walks the earth."

PUBLICATION HISTORY

To Love a Vampire was originally serialized in *Scary Monsters Magazine* from March 2011 to June 2013.

Printed in Great Britain
by Amazon

64617563R00132